CHRISTMAS STORIES

Selected by
GILES GORDON

First published 1995

Bloomsbury Publishing Plc, 2 Soho Square,
London WIV 6HB

A CIP catalogue record for this book is available
from the British Library

ISBN 0 7475 2312 6

10 9 8 7 6 5 4 3 2 1

Typeset by Hewer Text Composition Services, Edinburgh
Printed in Great Britain by St Edmundsbury Press, Suffolk
Jacket design by Jeff Fisher

CONTENTS

HANS ANDERSEN
The Fir-Tree

Far away in the deep forest there once grew a pretty Fir-Tree; the situation was delightful, the sun shone full upon him, the breeze played freely around him, and in the neighbourhood grew many companion fir-trees, some older, some younger. But the little Fir-Tree was not happy: he was always longing to be tall; he thought not of the warm sun and the fresh air; he cared not for the merry, prattling peasant children who came to the forest to look for strawberries and raspberries. Except, indeed, sometimes, when, after having filled their pitchers, or threaded the bright berries on a straw, they would sit down near the little Fir-Tree, and say, 'What a pretty little tree this is!' and then the Fir-Tree would feel very much vexed.

Year by year he grew, a long green shoot sent he forth every year; for you may always tell how many years a fir-tree has lived by counting the number of joints in its stem.

'Oh, that I was as tall as the others are,' sighed the little Tree, 'then I should spread out my branches so far, and my crown should look out over the wide world around! The birds would build their nests among my branches, and when the wind blew I should bend my head so grandly, just as the others do!'

He had no pleasure in the sunshine, in the song of the birds, or in the red clouds that sailed over him every morning and evening.

In the winter-time, when the ground was covered with the white, glistening snow, there was a hare that would come continually scampering about, and jumping right over the little Tree's head – and that was most provoking! However, two winters passed away, and by the third the Tree was so tall that the hare was obliged to run round it. 'Oh! to grow, to grow, to become tall and old, that is the only thing in the world worth living for' – so thought the Tree.

The wood-cutters came in the autumn and felled some among the largest of the trees; this happened every year, and our young Fir, who was by this time a tolerable height, shuddered when he saw those grand, magnificent trees fall with a tremendous crash, crackling to the earth: their boughs were then all cut off; terribly naked, and lanky, and long did the stems look after this – they could hardly be recognised. They were laid one upon another in waggons, and horses drew them away, far, far away, from the forest. Where could they be going? What might be their fortunes?

So next spring, when the Swallows and the Storks had returned from abroad, the Tree asked them, saying, 'Know you not whither they are taken? Have you not met them?'

The Swallows knew nothing about the matter, but the Stork looked thoughtful for a moment, then nodded his head, and said, 'Yes, I believe I have seen them! As I was flying from Egypt to this place I met several ships; those ships had splendid masts. I have little doubt that they were the trees that you speak of; they smelled like fir-wood. I may congratulate you, for they sailed gloriously, quite gloriously!'

'Oh, that I, too, were tall enough to sail upon the sea! Tell me what it is, this sea, and what it looks like.'

'Thank you, it would take too long, a great deal!' said the Stork, and away he stalked.

'Rejoice in thy youth!' said the Sunbeams; 'rejoice in thy luxuriant youth, in the fresh life that is within thee!'

And the Wind kissed the Tree, and the Dew wept tears over him, but the Fir-Tree understood them not.

When Christmas approached, many quite young trees were felled – trees which were some of them not so tall or of just the same height as the young restless Fir-Tree who was always longing to be away; these young trees were chosen from the most beautiful, their branches were not cut off, they were laid in a waggon, and horses drew them away, far, far away, from the forest.

'Where are they going?' asked the Fir-Tree. 'They are not larger than I am; indeed, one of them was much less; why do they keep all their branches? Where can they be gone?'

'We know! We know!' twittered the Sparrows. 'We peeped in through the windows of the town below! We know where they are gone! Oh, you cannot think what honour and glory they receive! We looked through the window-panes and saw them planted in a warm room, and decked out with such beautiful things – gilded apples, sweet-meats, playthings, and hundreds of bright candles!'

'And then?' asked the Fir-Tree, trembling in every bough; 'and then? What happened then?'

'Oh, we saw no more. That was beautiful, beautiful beyond compare!'

'Is this glorious lot destined to be mine?' cried the Fir-Tree, with delight. 'This is far better than sailing over the sea. How I long for the time! Oh, that Christmas were come! I am now tall and full of branches, like the others which last year were carried away. Oh, that I were even now in the waggon! That I were in the warm room, honoured and adorned! And then – yes, then, something still better must happen, else why should they take the trouble to decorate me? It must be that something still greater, still more splendid, must happen – but what? Oh, I suffer, I suffer with longing! I know not what it is that I feel!'

'Rejoice in our love!' said the Air and the Sunshine. 'Rejoice in thy youth and thy freedom!'

But rejoice he never would: he grew and grew, in winter as in summer; he stood there clothed in green, dark-green foliage; the people that saw him said, 'That is a beautiful tree!' and, next Christmas, he was the first that was felled. The axe struck sharply through the wood, the tree fell to the earth with a heavy groan; he suffered an agony, a faintness that he had never expected; he quite forgot to think of his good fortune, he felt such sorrow at being compelled to leave his home, the place whence he had sprung; he knew that he should never see again those dear old comrades, or the little bushes and flowers that had flourished under his shadow, perhaps not even the birds. Neither did he find the journey by any means pleasant.

The Tree first came to himself when, in the courtyard to which he was first taken with the other trees, he heard a man say, 'This is a splendid one, the very thing we want!'

Then came two smartly-dressed servants, and carried the Fir-Tree into a large and handsome saloon. Pictures hung on the walls, and on the mantelpiece stood large Chinese vases with lions on the lids; there were rocking-chairs, silken sofas, tables covered with picture-books, and toys that had cost a hundred times a hundred dollars – at least so said the children. And the Fir-Tree was planted in a large cask filled with sand, but no one could know that it was a cask, for it was hung with green cloth and placed upon a carpet woven of many gay colours. Oh, how the Tree trembled! What was to happen next? A young lady, assisted by the servants, now began to adorn him.

Upon some branches they hung little nets cut out of coloured paper, every net filled with sugar-plums; from others gilded apples and walnuts were suspended, looking just as if they had grown there; and more than a hundred little wax-tapers, red, blue, and white, were placed here and there among the boughs. Dolls, that looked almost like men and women – the Tree had never seen such things before – seemed dancing to and fro among the leaves, and highest, on the summit, was fastened a large star of gold tinsel; this was, indeed, splendid, splendid beyond compare! 'This evening,' they said, 'this evening it will be lighted up.'

'Would that it were evening!' thought the Tree. 'Would that the lights were kindled, for then – what will happen then? Will the trees come out of the forest to see me? Will the sparrows fly here and look in through the window-panes? Shall I stand here adorned both winter and summer?'

He thought much of it; he thought till he had bark-ache with longing, and bark-aches with trees are as bad as headaches with us. The candles were lighted – oh, what a blaze of splendour! The Tree trembled in all his branches, so that one of them caught fire. 'Oh, dear!' cried the young lady, and it was extinguished in great haste.

So the Tree dared not tremble again; he was so fearful of losing something of his splendour, he felt almost bewildered in the midst of all this glory and brightness. And now, all of a sudden, both folding-doors were flung open, and a troop of children rushed in as if they had a mind to jump over him; the older people followed more quietly; the little ones stood quite silent, but only for a moment! Then their jubilee burst forth afresh; they shouted till the walls re-echoed, they danced round the Tree, one present after another was torn down.

'What are they doing?' thought the Tree; 'what will happen now?' And the candles burned down to the branches, so they were extinguished – and the children were given leave to plunder the Tree. Oh! they rushed upon him in such riot that the boughs all crackled; had not his summit been festooned with the gold star to the ceiling he would have been overturned.

The children danced and played about with their beautiful playthings, no one thought any more of the Tree except the old nurse, who came and peeped among the boughs, but it was only to see whether perchance a fig or an apple had not been left among them.

'A story! A story!' cried the children, pulling a short thick man towards the tree. He sat down, saying, 'It is pleasant to sit under the shade of green boughs; besides, the Tree may be benefited by hearing my story. But I shall only tell you one. Would you like to hear about Ivedy Avedy, or about Humpty Dumpty, who fell downstairs, and yet came to the throne and won the Princess?'

'Ivedy Avedy!' cried some. 'Humpty Dumpty!' cried others; there was a famous uproar; the Fir-Tree alone was silent, thinking to himself, 'Ought I to make a noise as they do, or ought I to do nothing at all?' for he most certainly was one of the company, and had done all that had been required of him.

And the short thick man told the story of Humpty Dumpty, who fell downstairs, and yet came to the throne and won the Princess. And the children clapped their hands and called out for another; they wanted to hear the story of Ivedy Avedy also, but they did not get it. The Fir-Tree stood meanwhile quite silent and thoughtful – the birds in the forest had never related anything like this. 'Humpty Dumpty fell downstairs, and yet was raised to the throne and won the Princess! Yes, yes, strange things come to pass in the world!' thought the Fir-Tree, who believed it must all be true, because such a pleasant man had related it. 'Ah, ah! Who knows but I may fall downstairs and win a Princess?' And he rejoiced in the expectation of being next day again decked out with candles and playthings, gold and fruit.

'Tomorrow I will not tremble,' thought he. 'I will rejoice in my magnificence. Tomorrow I shall again hear the story of Humpty Dumpty, and perhaps that about Ivedy Avedy likewise.' And the Tree mused thereupon all night.

In the morning the maids came in.

'Now begins my state anew!' thought the Tree. But they dragged him out of the room, up the stairs, and into an attic-chamber, and there thrust him into a dark corner, where not a ray of light could penetrate. 'What can be the meaning of this?' thought the Tree. 'What am I to do here? What shall I hear in this place?' And he leant against the wall, and thought, and thought. And plenty of time he had for thinking it over, for day after day, and night after night, passed away, and yet no one ever came into the room. At last somebody did come in, but it was only to push into the corner some old trunks: the Tree was now entirely hidden from sight, and apparently entirely forgotten.

'It is now winter,' thought the Tree. 'The ground is hard and covered with snow; they cannot plant me now, so I am to stay here in shelter till the spring. Men are so clever and prudent! I only wish it were not so dark and so dreadfully lonely! Not even a little hare! Oh, how pleasant it was in the forest, when the snow lay on the ground and the hare scampered about – yes, even when he jumped over my head, though I did not like it then. It is so terribly lonely here.'

'Squeak! Squeak!' cried a little Mouse, just then gliding forward. Another followed; they snuffed about the Fir-Tree, and then slipped in and out among the branches.

'It is horribly cold!' said the little Mice. 'Otherwise it is very comfortable here. Don't you think so, you old Fir-Tree?'

'I am not old,' said the Fir-Tree; 'there are many who are much older than I am.'

'How came you here?' asked the Mice, 'and what do you know?' They were most uncommonly curious. 'Tell us about the most delightful place on earth! Have you ever been there? Have you been into the store-room, where cheeses lie on the shelves, and bacon hangs from the ceiling; where one can dance over tallow-candles; where one goes in thin and comes out fat?'

'I know nothing about that,' said the Tree, 'but I know the forest, where the sun shines and where the birds sing!' and then he spoke of his youth and its pleasures. The little Mice had never heard anything like it before; they listened so attentively and said, 'Well, to be sure! How much you have seen! How happy you have been!'

'Happy!' repeated the Fir-Tree, in surprise, and he thought a moment over all that he had been saying – 'Yes, on the whole, those were pleasant times!' He then told them about the Christmas Eve, when he had been decked out with cakes and candles.

'Oh!' cried the little Mice, 'how happy you have been, you old Fir-Tree!'

'I am not old at all!' returned the Fir; 'it is only this winter that I have left the forest; I am just in the prime of life!'

'How well you can talk!' said the little Mice; and the next night they came again, and brought with them four other little Mice, who wanted also to hear the Tree's history; and the more the Tree spoke of his youth in the forest, the more vividly he remembered it, and said, 'Yes, those were pleasant times! But they may come again, they may come again! Humpty Dumpty fell downstairs, and for all that he won the Princess; perhaps I, too, may win a Princess'; and then the Fir-Tree thought of a pretty little delicate Birch-Tree that grew in the forest – a real Princess, a very lovely Princess, was she to the Fir-Tree.

'Who is this Humpty Dumpty?' asked the little Mice. Whereupon he related the tale; he could remember every word of it perfectly: and the little Mice were ready to jump to the top of the Tree for joy. The night following several more Mice came, and on Sunday came also two Rats; they, however, declared that the story was not at all amusing, which much vexed the little Mice, who, after hearing their opinion, could not like it so well either.

'Do you know only that one story?' asked the Rats.

'Only that one!' answered the Tree; 'I heard it on the happiest evening of my life, though I did not then know how happy I was.'

'It is a miserable story! Do you know none about pork and tallow? – no store-room story?'

'No,' said the Tree.

'Well, then we have heard enough of it!' returned the Rats, and they went their ways.

The little Mice, too, never came again. The Tree sighed. 'It was pleasant when they sat round me, those busy little Mice, listening to my words. Now that, too, is all past! However, I shall have pleasure in remembering it, when I am taken away from this place.'

But when would that be? One morning, people came and routed out the lumber-room; the trunks were taken away, the Tree, too, was dragged out of the corner; they threw him carelessly on the floor, but one of the servants picked him up and carried him downstairs. Once more he beheld the light of day.

'Now life begins again!' thought the Tree; he felt the fresh air, the warm sunbeams – he was out in the court. All happened so quickly that the Tree quite forgot to look at himself – there was so much to look at all around. The court joined a garden, everything was so fresh and blooming, the roses clustered so bright and so fragrant round the trellis-work, the lime-trees were in full blossom, and the swallows flew backwards and forwards, twittering, 'Quirri-virri-vit, my beloved is come!' but it was not the Fir-Tree whom they meant.

'I shall live! I shall live!' He was filled with delightful hope; he tried to spread out his branches, but, alas! they were all dried up and yellow. He was thrown down upon a heap of weeds and nettles. The star of gold tinsel that had been left fixed on his crown now sparkled brightly in the sunshine.

Some merry children were playing in the court, the same who at Christmas-time had danced round the Tree. One of the youngest now perceived the gold star, and ran to tear it off.

'Look at it, still fastened to the ugly old Christmas-Tree!' cried he, trampling upon the boughs till they broke under his boots.

And the Tree looked on all the flowers of the garden now blooming in the freshness of their beauty; he looked upon himself, and he wished from his heart that he had been left to wither alone in the dark corner of the lumber-room: he called to mind his happy forest-life, the merry Christmas Eve, and the little Mice who had listened so eagerly when he related the story of Humpty Dumpty.

'Past, all past!' said the poor Tree. 'Had I but been happy, as I might have been! Past, all past!'

And the servant came and broke the Tree into small pieces, heaped them up and set fire to them. And the Tree groaned deeply, and every groan sounded like a little shot; the children all ran up to the place and jumped about in front of the blaze, looking into it and crying, 'Piff! piff!' But at each of those heavy groans the Fir-Tree thought of a bright summer's day, or a starry winter's night in the forest, of Christmas Eve, or of Humpty Dumpty, the only story that he knew and could relate. And at last the Tree was burned.

The boys played about in the court; on the bosom of the youngest sparkled the gold star that the Tree had worn on the happiest evening of his life; but that was past, and the Tree was past, and the story also, past! past! for all stories must come to an end, some time or other.

ELIZABETH BOWEN
The Cheery Soul

On arriving, I first met the aunt of whom they had told me, the aunt who had not yet got over being turned out of Italy. She sat resentfully by the fire, or rather the fireplace, and did not look up when I came in. The acrid smell that curled through the drawing-room could be traced to a grate full of sizzling fir cones that must have been brought in damp. From the mantelpiece one lamp, with its shade tilted, shed light on the parting of the aunt's hair. It could not be said that the room was cheerful: the high, curtained bow windows made draughty caves; the armchairs and sofas, pushed back against the wall, wore the air of being renounced for ever. Only a row of discreet greeting-cards (few with pictures) along the top of a bureau betrayed the presence of Christmas. There was no holly, and no pieces of string.

I coughed and said: 'I feel I should introduce myself,' and followed this up by giving the aunt my name, which she received with apathy. When she did stir, it was to look at the parcel that I coquettishly twirled from its loop of string. 'They're not giving presents, this year,' she said in alarm. 'If I were you, I should put that back in my room.'

'It's just – my rations.'

'In that case,' she remarked, 'I really don't know what you had better do.' Turning away from me she picked up a small bent poker, and with this began to interfere with the fir cones, of which several, steaming, bounced from the grate. 'A good wood stove,' she said, 'would make all the difference. At Sienna, though they say it is cold in winter, we never had troubles of this kind.'

'How would it be,' I said, 'if I sat down?' I pulled a chair a little on to the hearthrug, if only for the idea of the thing. 'I gather our hosts are out. I wonder where they have gone to?'

'Really, I couldn't tell you.'

'My behaviour,' I said, 'has been shockingly free-and-easy. Having pulled the bell three times, waited, had a go at the knocker . . .'

'. . . I heard,' she said, slightly bowing her head.

'I gave *that* up, tried the door, found it unlocked, so just marched in.'

'Have you come about something?' she said with renewed alarm.

'Well, actually, I fear that I've come to stay. They have been so very kind as to . . .'

'. . . Oh, I remember – someone *was* coming.' She looked at me rather closely. 'Have you been here before?'

'Never. So this is delightful,' I said firmly. 'I am billeted where I work' (I named the industrial town, twelve miles off, that was these days in a ferment of war production), 'my landlady craves my room for these next two days for her daughter, who is on leave, and, on top of this, to be frank, I'm a bit old-fashioned: Christmas alone in a strange town didn't appeal to me. So you can see how I sprang at . . .'

'Yes, I can see,' she said. With the tongs, she replaced the cones that had fallen out of the fire. 'At Orvieto,' she said, 'the stoves were so satisfactory that one felt no ill effects from the tiled floors.'

As I could think of nothing to add to this, I joined her in listening attentively to the hall clock. My entry into the drawing-room having been tentative, I had not made so bold as to close the door behind me, so a further coldness now seeped through from the hall. Except for the clock – whose loud tick was reluctant – there was not another sound to be heard: the very silence seemed to produce echoes. The Rangerton-Karneys' absence from their own house was becoming, virtually, ostentatious. 'I understand,' I said, 'that they are tremendously busy. Practically never not on the go.'

'They expect to have a finger in every pie.'

Their aunt's ingratitude shocked me. She must be (as they had hinted) in a difficult state. They had always spoken with the most marked forbearance of her enforced return to them out of Italy. In England, they said, she had no other roof but theirs, and they were constantly wounded (their friends told me) by her saying she would have preferred internment in Italy.

In common with all my fellow-workers at ——, I had a high regard for the Rangerton-Karneys, an admiration tempered, perhaps, with awe. Their energy in the promotion of every war effort was only matched by the austerity of their personal lives. They appeared to have given up almost everything. That they never sat down could be seen from their drawing-room chairs. As 'local people' of the most solid kind they were on terms with the bigwigs of every department, the key minds of our small but now rather important town. Completely discreet, they were palpably 'in the know'.

Their house in the Midlands, in which I now so incredibly found myself, was largish, built of the local stone, *circa* 1860 I should say from its style. It was not very far from a railway junction, and at a still less distance from a canal. I had evaded the strictures on Christmas travel by making the twelve-mile journey by bicycle – indeed, the suggestion that I should do this played a prominent part in their invitation. So I bicycled over. My little things for the two nights were contained in one of those useful American-cloth suitcases, strapped to my back-wheel carrier, while my parcel of rations could be slung, I found, from my handlebar. The bumping of this parcel on my right knee as I pedalled was a major embarrassment. To cap this, the misty damp of the afternoon had caused me to set off in a mackintosh. At the best of times I am not an expert cyclist. The grateful absence of hills (all this country is very flat) was cancelled out by the greasiness of the roads, and army traffic often made me dismount – it is always well to be on the safe side. Now and then, cows or horses loomed up abruptly to peer at me over the reeking hedgerows. The few anonymous villages I passed through all appeared, in the falling dusk, to be very much the same: their inhabitants wore an air of war-time discretion, so I did not dare risk snubs by asking how far I had come. My pocket map, however, proved less unhelpful when I found that I had been reading it upside down. When, about halfway, I turned on my lamp, I watched mist curdle under its wobbling ray. My spectacles dimmed steadily; my hands numbed inside my knitted gloves (the only Christmas present I had received so far) and the mist condensed on my muffler in fine drops.

I own that I had sustained myself through this journey on thoughts of the cheery welcome ahead. The Rangerton-Karneys' invitation, delivered by word of mouth only three days ago, had been totally unexpected, as well as gratifying. I had had no reason to think they had taken notice of me. We had met rarely, when I reported to the committees on which they sat. That the brother and two sisters (so much alike that people took them for triplets) had attracted *my* wistful notice, I need not say. But not only was my position a quite obscure one; I am not generally sought out; I make few new friends. None of my colleagues had been to the Rangerton-Karneys' house: there was an idea that they had given up guests. As the news of their invitation to me spread (and I cannot say I did much to stop it spreading) I rose rapidly in everyone's estimation.

In fact, their thought had been remarkably kind. Can you wonder that I felt myself favoured? I was soon, now, to see their erstwhile committee faces wreathed with seasonable and genial smiles. I never was one to doubt that people unbend at home. Perhaps a little feverish from my cycling, I pictured blazing hearths through holly-garlanded doors.

Owing to this indulgence in foolish fancy, my real arrival rather deflated me.

'I suppose they went out after tea?' I said to the aunt.

'After lunch, I think,' she replied. 'There was no tea.' She picked up her book, which was about Mantegna, and went on reading, pitched rather tensely forward to catch the light of the dim-bulbed lamp. I hesitated, then rose up, saying that perhaps I had better deliver my rations to the cook. 'If you can,' she said, turning over a page.

The whirr of the clock preparing to strike seven made me jump. The hall had funny acoustics – so much so that I strode across the wide breaches from rug to rug rather than hear my step on the stone flags. Draught and dark coming down a shaft announced the presence of stairs. I saw what little I saw by the flame of a night-light, palpitating under a blue glass inverted shade. The hall and the staircase windows were not blacked out yet. (Back in the drawing-room, I could only imagine, the aunt must have so far bestirred herself as to draw the curtains.)

The kitchen was my objective – as I had said to the aunt. I pushed at a promising baize door: it immediately opened upon a vibration of heat and rich, heartening smells. At these, the complexion of everything changed once more. If my spirits, just lately, had not been very high, this was no doubt due to the fact that I had lunched on a sandwich, then had not dared leave my bicycle to look for a cup of tea. I was in no mood to reproach the Rangerton-Karneys for this Christmas break in their well-known austere routine.

But, in view of this, the kitchen was a surprise. Warm, and spiced with excellent smells, it was in the dark completely but for the crimson glow from between the bars of the range. A good deal puzzled, I switched the light on – the black-out, here, had been punctiliously done.

The glare made me jump. The cook must have found, for her own use, a quadruple-power electric bulb. This now fairly blazed down on the vast scrubbed white wood table, scored and scarred by decades of the violent chopping of meat. I looked about – to be staggered by what I did not see. Neither on range, table, nor outsize dresser were there signs of the preparation of any meal. Not a plate, not a spoon, not a canister showed any signs of action. The heat-vibrating top of the range was bare; all the pots and pans were up above, clean and cold, in their places along the rack. I went so far as to open the oven door – a roasting smell came out, but there was nothing inside. A tap drip-drop-dripped on an upturned bowl in the sink – but nobody had been peeling potatoes there.

I put my rations down on the table and was, dumbfounded, preparing to turn away, when a white paper on the white wood caught my eye. This paper, in an inexpert line of block-printing, bore the somewhat unnecessary statement: I AM NOT HERE. To this was added, in brackets: 'Look in the fish kettle.' Though this be no affair of mine, could I fail to follow it up? Was this some new demonstration of haybox cookery; was I to find our dinner snugly concealed? I identified the fish kettle, a large tin object (about the size, I should say, of an infant's bath) that stood on a stool halfway between the sink and range. It wore a tight-fitting lid, which came off with a sort of plop: the sound in itself had an ominous hollowness. Inside, I found, again, only a piece of paper. This said: 'Mr & the 2 Misses Rangerton-Karney can boil their heads. This holds 3.'

I felt that the least I could do for my hosts the Rangerton-Karneys was to suppress this unkind joke, so badly out of accord with the Christmas spirit. I *could* have dropped the paper straight into the kitchen fire, but on second thoughts I went back to consult the aunt. I found her so very deep in Mantegna as to be oblivious of the passage of time. She clearly did not like being interrupted. I said: 'Can you tell me if your nephew and nieces had any kind of contretemps with their cook today?'

She replied: 'I make a point of not asking questions.'

'Oh, so do I,' I replied, 'in the normal way. But I fear . . .'

'You fear what?'

'She's gone,' I said. 'Leaving this . . .'

The aunt looked at the paper, then said: 'How curious.' She added: 'Of course, she has gone: that happened a year ago. She must have left several messages, I suppose. I remember that Etta found one in the mincing machine, saying to tell them to mince their gizzards. Etta seemed very much put out. That was *last* Christmas Eve, I remember – dear me, what a coincidence . . . So you found this, did you?' she said, re-reading the paper with less repugnance than I should have wished to see. 'I expect, if you went on poking about the kitchen . . .'

Annoyed, I said tartly: 'A reprehensible cook!'

'No worse than other English cooks,' she replied. 'They all declare they have never heard of a *pasta*, and that oil in cookery makes one repeat. But I always found her cheerful and kind. And of course I miss her – Etta's been cooking since.' (This was the elder Miss Rangerton-Karney.)

'But look,' I said, 'I was led to *this* dreadful message, by another one, on the table. *That* can't have been there a year.'

'I suppose not,' the aunt said, showing indifference. She picked up her book and inclined again to the lamp.

I said: 'You don't think some other servant . . .'

She looked at me like a fish.

'They *have* no other servants. Oh no: not since the cook . . .'

Her voice trailed away. 'Well, it's all very odd, I'm sure.'

'It's worse than odd, my dear lady: there won't be any dinner.'

She shocked me by emitting a kind of giggle. She said 'Unless they *do* boil their heads.'

The idea that the Rangerton-Karneys might be out on a cook-hunt rationalized this perplexing evening for me. I am always more comfortable when I can tell myself that people are, after all, behaving accountably. The Rangerton-Karneys always acted in trio. The idea that one of them should stay at home to receive me while the other two went ploughing round the dark country would, at this crisis, never present itself. The Rangerton-Karneys' three sets of thoughts and feelings always appeared to join at the one root: one might say that they had a composite character. One thing, I could reflect, about misadventures is that they make for talk and often end in a laugh. I tried in vain to picture the Rangerton-Karneys laughing – for that was a thing I had never seen.

But if Etta is now resigned to doing the cooking . . .? I thought better not to puzzle the thing out.

Screening my electric torch with my fingers past the uncurtained windows, I went upstairs to look for what might be my room. In my other hand I carried my little case – to tell the truth, I was anxious to change my socks. Embarking on a long passage, with doors ajar, I discreetly projected my torch into a number of rooms. All were cold; some were palpably slept in, others dismantled. I located the resting-places of Etta, Max and Paulina by the odour of tar soap, shoe-leather and boiled woollen underclothes that announced their presences in so many committee rooms. At an unintimate distance along the passage, the glint of my torch on Florentine bric-à-brac suggested the headquarters of the aunt. I did at last succeed, by elimination, in finding the spare room prepared for me. They had put me just across the way from their aunt. My torch and my touch revealed a made-up bed, draped in a glacial white starched quilt, two fringed towels straddling the water-jug, and virgin white mats to receive my brushes and comb. I successively bumped my knee (the knee still sore from the parcel) on two upright chairs. Yes, this must be the room for me. Oddly enough, it was much less cold than the others – but I did not think of that at the time. Having done what was necessary to the window, I lit up, to consider my new domain.

Somebody had been lying on my bed. When I rest during the day, I always remove the quilt, but whoever it was had neglected to do this. A deep trough, with a map of creases, appeared. The creases, however, did not extend far. Whoever it was had lain here in a contented stupor.

I worried – Etta might blame me. To distract my thoughts, I opened my little case and went to put my things on the dressing-table. The mirror was tilted upwards under the light, and something was written on it in soap: DEARIE, DON'T MIND ME. I at once went to the washstand, where the soap could be verified – it was a used cake, one corner blunted by writing. On my way back, I kicked over a black bottle, which, so placed on the floor as to be in easy reach from the bed, now gaily and noisily bowled away. It was empty – I had to admit that its contents, breathed out again, gave that decided character to my room.

The aunt was to be heard, pattering up the stairs. Was this belated hostess-ship on her part? She came into view of my door, carrying the night-light from the hall table. Giving me a modest, affronted look she said: 'I thought I'd tidy my hair.'

'The cook has been lying on my bed.'

'That would have been very possible, I'm afraid. She was often a little – if you know what I mean. But, she left last Christmas.'

'She's written something.'

'I don't see what one can do,' the aunt said, turning into her room. For my part, I dipped a towel into the jug and reluctantly tried to rub out the cook's message, but this only left a blur all over the glass. I applied to this the drier end of the towel. Oddly enough (perhaps) I felt fortified: this occult good feeling was, somehow, warming. The cook was supplying that touch of nature I had missed since crossing the Rangerton-Karneys' threshold. Thus, when I stepped back for another look at the mirror, I was barely surprised to find that a sprig of mistletoe had been twisted around the cord of the hanging electric light.

My disreputable psychic pleasure was to be interrupted. Downstairs, in the caves of the house, the front door bell jangled, then jangled again. This was followed by an interlude with the knocker: an imperious rat-a-tat-tat. I called across to the aunt: 'Ought one of us to go down? It might be a telegram.'

'I don't think so – why?'

We heard the glass door of the porch (the door through which I had made my so different entry) being rattled open; we heard the hall traversed by footsteps with the weight of authority. In response to a mighty '*Anyone there*?' I defied the aunt's judgement and went hurrying down. Coming on a policeman outlined in the drawing-room door, my first thought was that this must be about the black-out. I edged in, silent, just behind the policeman: he looked about him suspiciously, then saw me. 'And who might you be?' he said.

The bringing out of his notebook gave me stage fright during my first and other replies. I explained that the Rangerton-Karneys had asked me to come and stay.

'Oh, they did?' he said. 'Well, that is a laugh. Seen much of them?'

'Not so far.'

'Well, you won't.' I asked why: he ignored my question, asked for all my particulars, quizzed my identity card. 'I shall check up on all this,' he said heavily. 'So they asked you for Christmas, did they? And just *when*, may I ask, was this invitation issued?'

'Well, er – three days ago.'

This made me quite popular. He said: 'Much as I thought. Attempt to cover their tracks and divert suspicion. I daresay you blew off all round about them having asked you here?'

'I may have mentioned it to one or two friends.'

He looked pleased again and said: 'Just what they reckoned on. Not a soul was to guess they had planned to bolt. As for you – *you're* a cool hand, I must say. Just walked in, found the place empty and dossed down. Never once strike you there was anything fishy?'

'A good deal struck me,' I replied austerely. 'I took it, however, that my host and his sisters had been unexpectedly called out – perhaps to look for a cook.'

'Ah, cook,' he said. 'Now what brought that to your mind?'

'Her whereabouts seemed uncertain, if you know what I mean.'

Whereupon, he whipped over several leaves of his notebook. 'The last cook employed here,' he said, 'was in residence here four days, departing last Christmas Eve, December 24th, 194–. We have evidence that she stated locally that she was unable to tolerate certain goings-on. She specified interference in her department, undue advantage taken of the rationing system, mental cruelty to an elderly female refugee . . .'

I interposed: 'That would certainly be the aunt.'

'. . . and failure to observe Christmas in the appropriate manner. On this last point she expressed herself violently. She further adduced (though with less violence of feeling) that her three employers were "dirty spies, with their noses in everything". Subsequently, she withdrew this last remark; her words were, "I do not wish to make trouble, as I know how to make trouble in a way of my own." However, certain remarks she had let drop have been since followed up, and proved useful in our inquiries. Unhappily, we cannot check up on them, as the deceased met her end shortly after leaving this house.'

'The *deceased*?' I cried, with a sinking heart.

'Proceeding through the hall door and down the approach or avenue, in an almost total state of intoxication, she was heard singing "God rest you merry, gentlemen, let nothing you dismay". She also shouted: "Me for an English Christmas!" Accosting several pedestrians, she informed them that in her opinion times were not what they were. She spoke with emotion (being intoxicated) of turkey, mince pies, ham, plum pudding, etc. She was last seen hurrying in the direction of the canal, saying she must get brandy to make her sauce. She was last heard in the vicinity of the canal. The body was recovered from the canal on Boxing Day, December 26th, 194–.'

'But what,' I said, 'has happened to the Rangerton-Karneys?'

'Now, now!' said the policeman, shaking his finger sternly. 'You *may* hear as much as is good for you, one day – or you may not. Did you ever hear of the Safety of the Realm? I don't mind telling you one thing – you're lucky. You might have landed yourself in a nasty mess.'

'But, good heavens – the *Rangerton-Karneys*! They know everyone.'

'Ah,' he said, 'but it's that kind you have to watch.' Heavy with this reflection, his eye travelled over the hearthrug. He stooped with a creak and picked up the aunt's book. 'Wop name,' he said, 'propaganda: sticks out a mile. Now, don't you cut off anywhere, while I am now proceeding to search the house.'

'Cut off?' I nearly said. 'What do you take me for?' Alone, I sat down in the aunt's chair and dropped a few more fir cones into the extinct fire.

NATHANIEL HAWTHORNE
The Christmas Banquet

'I have here attempted,' said Roderick, unfolding a few sheets of manuscript, as he sat with Rosina and the sculptor in the summer-house, 'I have attempted to seize hold of a personage who glides past me, occasionally, in my walk through life. My former sad experience, as you know, has gifted me with some degree of insight into the gloomy mysteries of the human heart, through which I have wandered like one astray in a dark cavern, with his torch fast flickering to extinction. But this man, this class of men, is a hopeless puzzle.'

'Well, but propound him,' said the sculptor. 'Let us have an idea of him, to begin with.'

'Why, indeed,' replied Roderick, 'he is such a being as I could conceive you to carve out of marble, and some yet unrealized perfection of human science to endow with an exquisite mockery of intellect; but still there lacks the last inestimable touch of a divine Creator. He looks like man; and, perchance, like a better specimen of man than you ordinarily meet. You might esteem him wise; he is capable of cultivation and refinement, and has at least an external conscience; but the demands that spirit makes upon spirit are precisely those to which he cannot respond. When at last you come close to him you find him chill and unsubstantial – a mere vapour.'

'I believe,' said Rosina, 'I have a glimmering idea of what you mean.'

'Then be thankful,' answered her husband, smiling; 'but do not anticipate any further illumination from what I am about to read. I have here imagined such a man to be – what, probably, he never is – conscious of the deficiency in his spiritual organization. Methinks the result would be a sense of cold unreality wherewith he would go shivering through the world, longing to exchange his load of ice for any burden of real grief that fate could fling upon a human being.'

Contenting himself with this preface, Roderick began to read.

In a certain old gentleman's last will and testament there appeared a bequest, which, as his final thought and deed, was singularly in keeping with a long life of melancholy eccentricity. He devised a considerable sum for establishing a fund, the interest of which was to be expended annually for ever, in preparing a Christmas Banquet for ten of the most miserable persons that could be found. It seemed not to be the testator's purpose to make these half a score of sad hearts merry, but to provide that the stern or fierce expression of human discontent should not be drowned, even for that one holy and joyful day, amid the acclamations of festal gratitude which all Christendom sends up. And he desired, likewise, to perpetuate his own remonstrance against the earthly course of Providence, and his sad and sour dissent from those systems of religion or philosophy which either find sunshine in the world or draw it down from heaven.

The task of inviting the guests, or of selecting among such as might advance their claims to partake of this dismal hospitality, was confided to the two trustees or stewards of the fund. These gentlemen, like their deceased friend, were sombre humorists, who made it their principal occupation to number the sable threads in the web of human life, and drop all the golden ones out of the reckoning. They performed their present office with integrity and judgement. The aspect of the assembled company, on the day of the first festival, might not, it is true, have satisfied every beholder that these were especially the individuals, chosen forth from all the world, whose griefs were worthy to stand as indicators of the mass of human suffering. Yet after due consideration, it could not be disputed that here was a variety of hopeless discomfort, which, if it sometimes arose from causes apparently inadequate, was thereby only the shrewder imputation against the nature and mechanism of life.

The arrangements and decorations of the banquet were probably intended to signify that death in life which had been the testator's definition of existence. The hall, illuminated by torches, was hung round with curtains of deep and dusky purple, and adorned with branches of cypress and wreaths of artificial flowers, imitative of such as used to be strewn over the dead. A sprig of parsley was laid by every plate. The main reservoir of wine was a sepulchral urn of silver, whence the liquor was distributed around the table in small vases, accurately copied from those that held tears of ancient mourners. Neither had the stewards – if it were their taste that arranged these details – forgotten the fantasy of the old Egyptians, who seated a skeleton at every festive board, and mocked their own merriment with the imperturbable grin of a death's-head. Such a fearful guest, shrouded in a black mantle, sat now at the head of the table. It was whispered, I know not with what truth, that the testator himself had once walked the visible world with the machinery of that same skeleton, and that it was one of the stipulations of his will, that he should thus be permitted to sit, from year to year, at the banquet which he had instituted. If so, it was perhaps covertly implied that he had cherished no hopes of bliss beyond the grave to compensate for the evils which he felt or imagined here. And if, in their bewildered conjectures as to the purpose of earthly existence, the banqueters should throw aside the veil, and cast an inquiring glance at this figure of death, as seeking thence the solution otherwise unattainable, the only reply would be a stare of the vacant eye caverns and a grin of the skeleton jaws. Such was the response that the dead man had fancied himself to receive when he asked of Death to solve the riddle of his life; and it was his desire to repeat it when the guests of his dismal hospitality should find themselves perplexed with the same question.

'What means that wreath?' asked several of the company, while viewing the decorations of the table.

They alluded to a wreath of cypress, which was held on high by a skeleton arm, protruding from within the black mantle.

'It is a crown,' said one of the stewards, 'not for the worthiest, but for the woefulest, when he shall prove his claim to it.'

The guest earliest bidden to the festival was a man of soft and gentle character, who had not energy to struggle against the heavy despondency to which his temperament rendered him liable; and therefore with nothing outwardly to excuse him from happiness, he had spent a life of quiet misery that made his blood torpid, and weighed upon his breath, and sat like a ponderous night-fiend upon every throb of his unresisting heart. His wretchedness seemed as deep as his original nature, if not identical with it. It was the misfortune of a second guest to cherish within his bosom a diseased heart, which had become so wretchedly sore that the continual and unavoidable rubs of the world, the blow of an enemy, the careless jostle of a stranger, and even the faithful and loving touch of a friend, alike made ulcers in it. As is the habit of people thus afflicted, he found his chief employment in exhibiting these miserable sores to any who would give themselves the pain of viewing them. A third guest was a hypochondriac, whose imagination wrought necromancy in his outward and inward world, and caused him to see monstrous faces in the household fire, and dragons in the clouds of sunset, and fiends in the guise of beautiful women, and something ugly or wicked beneath all the pleasant surfaces of nature. His neighbour at table was one who, in his early youth, had trusted mankind too much, and hoped too highly in their behalf, and, in meeting with many disappointments, had become desperately soured. For several years back this misanthrope had employed himself in accumulating motives for hating and despising his race – such as murder, lust, treachery, ingratitude, faithlessness of trusted friends, instinctive vices of children, impurity of women, hidden guilt in men of saint-like aspect – and, in short, all manner of black realities that sought to decorate themselves with outward grace or glory. But at every atrocious fact that was added to his catalogue, at every increase of the sad knowledge which he spent his life to collect, the native impulses of the poor man's loving and confiding heart made him groan with anguish. Next, with his heavy brow bent downward, there stole into the hall a man naturally earnest and impassioned, who, from his immemorial infancy, had felt the consciousness of a high message to the world; but, essaying to deliver it, had found either no voice or form of speech, or else no ears to listen. Therefore his whole life was a bitter questioning of himself: 'Why have not men acknowledged my mission? Am I not a self-deluding fool? What business have I on earth? Where is my grave?' Throughout the festival, he quaffed frequent draughts from the sepulchral urn of wine, hoping thus to quench the celestial fire that tortured his own breast and could not benefit his race.

Then there entered, having flung away a ticket for a ball, a gay gallant of yesterday, who had found four or five wrinkles in his brow, and more grey hairs than he could well number on his head. Endowed with sense and feeling, he had nevertheless spent his youth in folly, but had reached at last that dreary point in life where Folly quits us of her own accord, leaving us to make friends with Wisdom if we can. Thus, cold and desolate, he had come to seek Wisdom at the banquet, and wondered if the skeleton were she. To eke out the company, the stewards had invited a distressed poet from his home in the almshouse, and a melancholy idiot from the street-corner. The latter had just the glimmering of sense that was sufficient to make him conscious of a vacancy, which the poor fellow, all his life long, had mistily sought to fill up with intelligence, wandering up and down the streets, and groaning miserably because his attempts were ineffectual. The only lady in the hall was one who had fallen short of absolute and perfect beauty, merely by the trifling defect of a slight cast in her left eye. But this blemish, minute as it was, so shocked the pure ideal of her soul, rather than her vanity, that she passed her life in solitude, and veiled her countenance even from her own gaze. So the skeleton sat shrouded at one end of the table, and this poor lady at the other.

One other guest remains to be described. He was a young man of smooth brow, fair cheeks, and fashionable mien. So far as his exterior developed him, he might much more suitably have found a place at some merry Christmas table, than have been numbered among the blighted, fate-stricken, fancy-tortured set of ill-starred banqueters. Murmurs arose among the guests as they noted the glance of general scrutiny which the intruder threw over his companions. What had he to do among them? Why did not the skeleton of the dead founder of the feast unbend its rattling joints, arise, and motion the unwelcome stranger from the board?

'Shameful!' said the morbid man, while a new ulcer broke out in his heart. 'He comes to mock us! – we shall be the jest of his tavern friends! – he will make a farce of our miseries, and bring it out upon the stage!'

'Oh, never mind him!' said the hypochondriac, smiling sourly. 'He shall feast from yonder tureen of viper-soup; and if there is a fricassee of scorpions on the table, pray let him have his share of it. For the dessert, he shall taste the apples of Sodom. Then, if he like our Christmas fare, let him return again next year!'

'Trouble him not,' murmured the melancholy man, with gentleness. 'What matters it whether the consciousness of misery come a few years sooner or later? If this youth deem himself happy now, yet let him sit with us for the sake of the wretchedness to come.'

The poor idiot approached the young man with that mournful aspect of vacant inquiry which his face continually wore, and which caused people to say that he was always in search of his missing wits. After no little examination he touched the stranger's hand, but immediately drew back his own, shaking his head and shivering.

'Cold, cold, cold!' muttered the idiot.

The young man shivered too, and smiled.

'Gentlemen, and you, madam,' said one of the stewards of the festival, 'do not conceive so ill either of our caution or judgement, as to imagine that we have admitted this young stranger – Gervayse Hastings by name – without a full investigation and thoughtful balance of his claims. Trust me, not a guest at the table is better entitled to his seat.'

The steward's guaranty was perforce satisfactory. The company, therefore, took their places, and addressed themselves to the serious business of the feast, but were soon disturbed by the hypochondriac, who thrust back his chair, complaining that a dish of stewed toads and vipers was set before him, and that there was green ditchwater in his cup of wine. This mistake being amended, he quietly resumed his seat. The wine, as it flowed freely from the sepulchral urn, seemed to come imbued with all gloomy inspirations; so that its influence was not to cheer, but either to sink the revellers into a deeper melancholy, or elevate their spirits to an enthusiasm of wretchedness. The conversation was various. They told sad stories about people who might have been worthy guests at such a festival as the present. They talked of grisly incidents in human history; of strange crimes, which, if truly considered were but convulsions of agony; of some lives that had been altogether wretched, and of others which, wearing a general semblance of happiness, had yet been deformed, sooner or later, by misfortune, as by the intrusion of a grim face at a banquet; of deathbed scenes, and what dark intimations might be gathered from the words of dying men; of suicide, and whether the more eligible mode were by halter, knife, poison, drowning, gradual starvation, or the fumes of charcoal. The majority of the guests, as is the custom with people thoroughly and profoundly sick at heart, were anxious to make their own woes the theme of discussion, and prove themselves most excellent in anguish. The misanthropist went deep into the philosophy of evil, and wandered about in the darkness, with now and then a gleam of discoloured light hovering on ghastly shapes and horrid scenery. Many a miserable thought, such as men have stumbled upon from age to age, did he now rake up again, and gloat over it as an inestimable gem, a diamond, a treasure far preferable to those bright, spiritual revelations of a better world, which are like precious stones from heaven's pavement. And then, amid his lore of wretchedness he hid his face and wept.

It was a festival at which the woful man of Uz might suitably have been a guest, together with all, in each succeeding age, who have tasted deepest of the bitterness of life. And be it said, too, that every son or daughter of woman, however favoured with happy fortune, might, at one sad moment or another, have claimed the privilege of a stricken heart, to sit down at this table. But throughout the feast it was remarked that the young stranger, Gervayse Hastings, was unsuccessful in his attempts to catch its pervading spirit. At any deep, strong thought that found utterance, and which was torn out, as it were, from the saddest recesses of human consciousness, he looked mystified and bewildered; even more than the poor idiot, who seemed to grasp at such things with his earnest heart, and thus occasionally to comprehend them. The young man's conversation was of a colder and lighter kind, often brilliant, but lacking the powerful characteristics of a nature that had been developed by suffering.

'Sir,' said the misanthropist, bluntly, in reply to some observation by Gervayse Hastings, 'pray do not address me again. We have no right to talk together. Our minds have nothing in common. By what claim you appear at this banquet I cannot guess; but methinks, to a man who could say what you have just now said, my companions and myself must seem no more than shadows flickering on the wall. And precisely such a shadow are you to us.'

The young man smiled and bowed, but, drawing himself back in his chair, he buttoned his coat over his breast, as if the banqueting-hall were growing chill. Again the idiot fixed his melancholy stare upon the youth, and murmured, 'Cold! cold! cold!'

The banquet drew to its conclusion, and the guests departed. Scarcely had they stepped across the threshold of the hall, when the scene that had there passed seemed like the vision of a sick fancy, or an exhalation from a stagnant heart. Now and then, however, during the year that ensued, these melancholy people caught glimpses of one another, transient, indeed, but enough to prove that they walked the earth with the ordinary allotment of reality. Sometimes a pair of them came face to face, while stealing through the evening twilight, enveloped in their sable cloaks. Sometimes they casually met in churchyards. Once, also, it happened that two of the dismal banqueters mutually started at recognizing each other in the noonday sunshine of a crowded street, stalking there like ghosts astray. Doubtless they wondered why the skeleton did not come abroad at noonday too.

But whenever the necessity of their affairs compelled these Christmas guests into the bustling world, they were sure to encounter the young man who had so unaccountably been admitted to the festival. They saw him among the gay and fortunate; they caught the sunny sparkle of his eye; they heard the light and careless tones of his voice, and muttered to themselves with such indignation as only the aristocracy of wretchedness could kindle, 'The traitor! The vile impostor! Providence, in its own good time, may give him a right to feast among us!' But the young man's unabashed eye dwelt upon their gloomy figures as they passed him, seeming to say, perchance with somewhat of a sneer, 'First, know my secret! – then, measure your claims with mine!'

The steps of Time stole onward, and soon brought merry Christmas round again, with glad and solemn worship in the churches, and sports, games, festivals, and everywhere the bright face of Joy beside the household fire. Again likewise the hall, with its curtains of dusky purple, was illuminated by the death-torches gleaming on the sepulchral decorations of the banquet. The veiled skeleton sat in state, lifting the cypress-wreath above its head, as the guerdon of some guest illustrious in the qualifications which there claimed precedence. As the stewards deemed the world inexhaustible in misery, and were desirous of recognizing it in all its forms, they had not seen fit to reassemble the company of the former year. New faces now threw their gloom across the table.

There was a man of nice conscience, who bore a bloodstain in his heart – the death of a fellow-creature – which, for his more exquisite torture, had chanced with such a peculiarity of circumstances, that he could not absolutely determine whether his will had entered into the deed or not. Therefore his whole life was spent in the agony of an inward trial for murder, with a continual sifting of the details of his terrible calamity, until his mind had no longer any thought, nor his soul any emotion, disconnected with it. There was a mother, too – a mother once, but a desolation now – who, many years before, had gone out on a pleasure-party, and, returning, found her infant smothered in its little bed. And ever since she has been tortured with the fantasy that her buried baby lay smothering in its coffin. Then there was an aged lady, who had lived from time immemorial with a constant tremor quivering through her fame. It was terrible to discern her dark shadow tremulous upon the wall; her lips, likewise, were tremulous; and the expression of her eye seemed to indicate that her soul was trembling too. Owing to the bewilderment and confusion which made almost a chaos of her intellect, it was impossible to discover what dire misfortune had thus shaken her nature to its depths; so that the stewards had admitted her to the table, not from any acquaintance with her history, but on the safe testimony of her miserable aspect. Some surprise was expressed at the presence of a bluff, red-faced gentleman, a certain Mr Smith, who had evidently the fat of many a rich feast within him, and the habitual twinkle of whose eye betrayed a disposition to break forth into uproarious laughter for little cause or none. It turned out, however, that, with the best possible flow of spirits, our poor friend was afflicted with a physical disease of the heart, which threatened instant death on the slightest cachinnatory indulgence, or even that titillation of the bodily frame produced by merry thoughts. In this dilemma he had sought admittance to the banquet, on the ostensible plea of his irksome and miserable state, but, in reality, with the hope of imbibing a life-preserving melancholy.

A married couple had been invited from a motive of bitter humour, it being well understood that they rendered each other unutterably miserable whenever they chanced to meet, and therefore must necessarily be fit associates at the festival. In contrast with these was another couple still unmarried, who had interchanged their hearts in early life, but had been divided by circumstances as impalpable as morning mist, and kept apart so long that their spirits now found it impossible to meet. Therefore, yearning for communion, yet shrinking from one another and choosing none beside, they felt themselves companionless in life, and looked upon eternity as a boundless desert. Next to the skeleton sat a mere son of earth – a hunter of the Exchange – a gatherer of shining dust – a man whose life's record was in his ledger, and whose soul's prison-house the vaults of the bank where he kept his deposits. This person had been greatly perplexed at his invitation, deeming himself one of the most fortunate men in the city; but the stewards persisted in demanding his presence, assuring him that he had no conception how miserable he was.

And now appeared a figure which we must acknowledge as our acquaintance of the former festival. It was Gervayse Hastings, whose presence had then caused so much question and criticism, and who now took his place with the composure of one whose claims were satisfactory to himself and must needs be allowed by others. Yet his easy and unruffled face betrayed no sorrow. The well-skilled beholders gazed a moment into his eyes and shook their heads, to miss the unuttered sympathy – the countersign never to be falsified – of those whose hearts are cavern-mouths through which they descend into a region of illimitable woe and recognize other wanderers there.

'Who is this youth?' asked the man with a bloodstain on his conscience. 'Surely he has never gone down into the depths! I know all the aspects of those who have passed through the dark valley. By what right is he among us?'

'Ah, it is a sinful thing to come hither without a sorrow,' murmured the aged lady, in accents that partook of the eternal tremor which pervaded her whole being. 'Depart, young man! Your soul has never been shaken, and, therefore, I tremble so much the more to look at you.'

'His soul shaken! No; I'll answer for it,' said bluff Mr Smith, pressing his hand upon his heart and making himself as melancholy as he could, for fear of a fatal explosion of laughter. 'I know the lad well; he has as fair prospects as any young man about town, and has no more right among us miserable creatures than the child unborn. He never was miserable, and probably never will be!'

'Our honoured guests,' interposed the stewards, 'pray have patience with us, and believe, at least, that our deep veneration for the sacredness of this solemnity would preclude any wilful violation of it. Receive this young man to your table. It may not be too much to say, that no guest here would exchange his own heart for the one that beats within that youthful bosom!'

'I'd call it a bargain, and gladly, too,' muttered Mr Smith, with a perplexing mixture of sadness and mirthful conceit. 'A plague upon their nonsense! My own heart is the only really miserable one in the company; it will certainly be the death of me at last!'

Nevertheless, as on the former occasion, the judgement of the stewards being without appeal, the company sat down. The obnoxious guest made no more attempt to obtrude his conversation on those about him, but appeared to listen to the table-talk with peculiar assiduity, as if some inestimable secret, otherwise beyond his reach, might be conveyed in a casual word. And in truth, to those who could understand and value it, there was rich matter in the upgushings and outpourings of these initiated souls to whom sorrow had been a talisman, admitting them into spiritual depths which no other spell can open. Sometimes out of the midst of densest gloom there flashed a momentary radiance, pure as crystal, bright as the flame of stars, and shedding such a glow upon the mysteries of life, that the guests were ready to exclaim, 'Surely the riddle is on the point of being solved!' At such illuminated intervals the saddest mourners felt it to be revealed that mortal griefs are but shadowy and external; no more than the sable robes voluminously shrouding a certain divine reality, and thus indicating what might otherwise be altogether invisible to mortal eye.

'Just now,' remarked the trembling old woman, 'I seemed to see beyond the outside. And then my everlasting tremor passed away!'

'Would that I could dwell always in these momentary gleams of light!' said the man of stricken conscience. 'Then the bloodstain in my heart would be washed clean away.'

This strain of conversation appeared so unintelligibly absurd to good Mr Smith, that he burst into precisely the fit of laughter which his physicians had warned him against, as likely to prove instantaneously fatal. In effect, he fell back in his chair a corpse, with a broad grin upon his face, while his ghost, perchance, remained beside it bewildered at its unpremeditated exit. This catastrophe of course broke up the festival.

'How is this? You do not tremble!' observed the tremulous old woman to Gervayse Hastings, who was gazing at the dead man with singular intentness. 'Is it not awful to see him so suddenly vanish out of the midst of life – this man of flesh and blood, whose earthly nature was so warm and strong? There is a never-ending tremor in my soul, but it trembles afresh at this! And you are calm!'

'Would that he could teach me somewhat!' said Gervayse Hastings, drawing a long breath. 'Men pass before me like shadows on the wall; their actions, passions, feelings, are flickerings of the light, and then they vanish! Neither the corpse, nor yonder skeleton, nor this old woman's everlasting tremor, can give me what I seek.'

And then the company departed.

We cannot linger to narrate, in such detail, more circumstances of these singular festivals, which, in accordance with the founder's will, continued to be kept with the regularity of an established institution. In process of time the stewards adopted the custom of inviting, from far and near, those individuals whose misfortunes were prominent above other men's, and whose mental and moral development might, therefore, be supposed to possess a corresponding interest. The exiled noble of the French Revolution and the broken soldier of the Empire were alike represented at the table. Fallen monarchs, wandering about the earth, have found places at that forlorn and miserable feast. The statesman, when his party flung him off, might, if he chose it, be once more a great man for the space of a single banquet. Aaron Burr's name appears on the record at a period when his ruin – the profoundest and most striking, with more of moral circumstance in it than that of almost any other man – was complete in his lonely age. Stephen Girard, when his wealth weighed upon him like a mountain, once sought admittance of his own accord. It is not probable, however, that these men had any lesson to teach in the lore of discontent and misery which might not equally well have been studied in the common walks of life. Illustrious unfortunates attract a wider sympathy, not because their griefs are more intense, but because, being set on lofty pedestals, they the better serve mankind as instances and bywords of calamity.

It concerns our present purpose to say that, at each successive festival, Gervayse Hastings showed his face, gradually changing from the smooth beauty of his youth to the thoughtful comeliness of manhood, and thence to the bald, impressive dignity of age. He was the only individual invariably present. Yet on every occasion there were murmurs, both from those who knew his character and position, and from them whose hearts shrank back as denying his companionship in their mystic fraternity.

'Who is this impassive man?' had been asked a hundred times. 'Has he suffered? Has he sinned? There are no traces of either. Then wherefore is he here?'

'You must inquire of the stewards or of himself,' was the constant reply. 'We seem to know him well here in our city, and know nothing of him but what is creditable and fortunate. Yet hither he comes, year after year, to this gloomy banquet, and sits among the guests like a marble statue. Ask yonder skeleton, perhaps that may solve the riddle!'

It was in truth a wonder. The life of Gervayse Hastings was not merely a prosperous, but a brilliant one. Everything had gone well with him. He was wealthy, far beyond the expenditure that was required by habits of magnificence, a taste of rare purity and cultivation, a love of travel, a scholar's instinct to collect a splendid library, and, moreover, what seemed a magnificent liberality to the distressed. He had sought happiness, and not vainly, if a lovely and tender wife, and children of fair promise, could ensure it. He had, besides, ascended above the limit which separates the obscure from the distinguished, and had won a stainless reputation in affairs of the widest public importance. Not that he was a popular character, or had within him the mysterious attributes which are essential to that species of success. To the public he was a cold abstraction, wholly destitute of those rich hues of personality, that living warmth, and the peculiar faculty of stamping his own heart's impression on a multitude of hearts, by which the people recognize their favourites. And it must be owned that, after his most intimate associates had done their best to know him thoroughly, and love him warmly, they were startled to find how little hold he had upon their affections. They approved, they admired, but still in those moments when the human spirit most craves reality, they shrank back from Gervayse

Hastings, as powerless to give them what they sought. It was the feeling of distrustful regret with which we should draw back the hand after extending it, in an illusive twilight, to grasp the hand of a shadow upon the wall.

As the superficial fervency of youth decayed, this peculiar effect of Gervayse Hastings's character grew more perceptible. His children, when he extended his arms, came coldly to his knees, but never climbed them of their own accord. His wife wept secretly, and almost adjudged herself a criminal because she shivered in the chill of his bosom. He, too, occasionally appeared not unconscious of the chillness of his moral atmosphere, and willing, if it might be so, to warm himself at a kindly fire. But age stole onward and benumbed him more and more. As the hoarfrost began to gather on him his wife went to her grave, and was doubtless warmer there; his children either died or were scattered to different homes of their own; and old Gervayse Hastings, unscathed by grief – alone, but needing no companionship – continued his steady walk through life, and still on every Christmas day attended at the dismal banquet. His privilege as a guest had become prescriptive now. Had he claimed the head of the table, even the skeleton would have been ejected from its seat.

Finally, at the merry Christmas-tide, when he had numbered fourscore years complete, this pale, high-browed, marble-featured old man once more entered the long-frequented hall, with the same impassive aspect that had called forth so much dissatisfied remark at his first attendance. Time, except in matters merely external, had done nothing for him, either of good or evil. As he took his place he threw a calm, inquiring glance around the table, as if to ascertain whether any guest had yet appeared, after so many unsuccessful banquets, who might impart to him the mystery – the deep, warm secret – the life within the life – which, whether manifested in joy or sorrow, is what gives substance to a world of shadows.

'My friends,' said Gervayse Hastings, assuming a position which his long conversance with the festival caused to appear natural, 'you are welcome! I drink to you all in this cup of sepulchral wine.'

The guests replied courteously, but still in a manner that proved them unable to receive the old man as a member of their sad fraternity. It may be well to give the reader an idea of the present company at the banquet.

One was formerly a clergyman, enthusiastic in his profession, and apparently of the genuine dynasty of those old Puritan divines whose faith in their calling, and stern exercise of it, had placed them among the mighty of the earth. But yielding to the speculative tendency of the age, he had gone astray from the firm foundation of an ancient faith, and wandered into a cloud-region, where everything was misty and deceptive, ever mocking him with a semblance of reality, but still dissolving when he flung himself upon it for support and rest. His instinct and early training demanded something steadfast; but, looking forward, he beheld vapours piled on vapours, and behind him an impassable gulf between the man of yesterday and today, on the borders of which he paced to and fro, sometimes wringing his hands in agony, and often making his own woe a theme of scornful merriment. This surely was a miserable man. Next, there was a theorist – one of a numerous tribe, although he deemed himself unique since the creation – a theorist, who had conceived a plan by which all the wretchedness of earth, moral and physical, might be done away, and the bliss of the millennium at once accomplished. But, the incredulity of mankind debarring him from action, he was smitten with as much grief as if the whole mass of woe which he was denied the opportunity to remedy were crowded into his own bosom. A plain old man in black attracted much of the company's notice, on the supposition that he was no other than Father Miller, who, it seemed, had given himself up to despair at the tedious delay of the final conflagration. Then there was a man distinguished for native pride and obstinacy, who, a little while before, had possessed immense wealth, and held the control of a vast moneyed interest which he had wielded in the same spirit as a despotic monarch would wield the power of his empire, carrying on a tremendous moral warfare, the roar and tremor of which was felt at every fireside in the land. At length came a crushing ruin – a total overthrow of fortune, power, and character – the effect of which on his imperious and, in many respects, noble and lofty nature might have entitled him to a place, not merely at our festival, but among the peers of Pandemonium.

There was a modern philanthropist, who had become so deeply sensible of the calamities of thousands and millions of his fellow-creatures, and of the impracticableness of any general measures for their relief, that he had no heart to do what little good lay immediately within his power, but contented himself with being miserable for sympathy. Near him sat a gentleman in a predicament hitherto unprecedented, but of which the present epoch probably affords numerous examples. Ever since he was of capacity to read a newspaper, this person had prided himself on his consistent adherence to one political party, but, in the confusion of these latter days, had got bewildered and knew not whereabouts his party was. This wretched condition, so morally desolate and disheartening to a man who has long accustomed himself to merge his individuality in the mass of a great body, can only be conceived by such as have experienced it. His next companion was a popular orator who had lost his voice, and – as it was pretty much all that he had to lose – had fallen into a state of hopeless melancholy. The table was likewise graced by two of the gentler sex – one, a half-starved, consumptive seamstress, the representative of thousands just as wretched; the other, a woman of unemployed energy, who found herself in the world with nothing to achieve, nothing to enjoy, and nothing even to suffer. She had, therefore, driven herself to the verge of madness by dark broodings over the wrongs of her sex, and its exclusion from a proper field of action. The roll of guests being thus complete, a side-table had been set for three or four disappointed office-seekers, with hearts as sick as death, whom the stewards had admitted partly because their calamities really entitled them to entrance here, and partly that they were in especial need of a good dinner. There was likewise a homeless dog, with his tail between his legs, licking up the crumbs and gnawing the fragments of the feast – such a melancholy cur as one sometimes sees about the streets without a master, and willing to follow the first that will accept his service.

In their own way, there were as wretched a set of people as ever had assembled at the festival.

There they sat, with the veiled skeleton of the founder holding aloft the cypress wreath, at one end of the table, and at the other, wrapped in furs, the withered figure of Gervayse Hastings, stately, calm, and cold, impressing the company with awe, yet so little interesting their sympathy that he might have vanished into thin air without their once exclaiming, 'Whither is he gone?'

'Sir,' said the philanthropist, addressing the old man, 'you have been so long a guest at this annual festival, and have thus been conversant with so many varieties of human affliction, that, not improbably, you have thence derived some great and important lessons. How blessed were your lot could you reveal a secret by which all this mass of woe might be removed!'

'I know of but one misfortune,' answered Gervayse Hastings, quietly, 'and that is my own.'

'Your own!' rejoined the philanthropist. 'And looking back on your serene and prosperous life, how can you claim to be the sole unfortunate of the human race?'

'You will not understand it,' replied Gervayse Hastings, feebly, and with a singular inefficiency of pronunciation, and sometimes putting one word for another. 'None have understood it, not even those who experience the like. It is a chillness, a want of earnestness, a feeling as if what should be my heart were a thing of vapour, a haunting perception of unreality! Thus seeming to possess all that other men have, all that men aim at, I have really possessed nothing, neither joy nor griefs. All things, all persons – as was truly said to me at this table long and long ago – have been like shadows flickering on the wall. It was so with my wife and children, with those who seemed my friends: it is so with yourselves, whom I see now before me. Neither have I myself any real existence, but am a shadow like the rest.'

'And how is it with your views of a future life?' inquired the speculative clergyman.

'Worse than with you,' said the old man, in a hollow and feeble tone; 'for I cannot conceive it earnestly enough to feel either hope or fear. Mine, – mine is the wretchedness! This cold heart – this unreal life! Ah! it grows colder still.'

It so chanced that at this juncture the decayed ligaments of the skeleton gave way, and the dry bones fell together in a heap, thus causing the dusty wreath of cypress to drop upon the table. The attention of the company being thus diverted for a single instant from Gervayse Hastings, they perceived, on turning again towards him, that the old man had undergone a change. His shadow had ceased to flicker on the wall.

'Well, Rosina, what is your criticism?' asked Roderick, as he rolled up the manuscript.

'Frankly, your success is by no means complete,' replied she. 'It is true, I have an idea of the character you endeavour to describe; but it is rather by dint of my own thought than your expression.'

'That is unavoidable,' observed the sculptor, 'because the characteristics are all negative. If Gervayse Hastings could have imbibed one human grief at the gloomy banquet, the task of describing him would have been infinitely easier. Of such persons – and we do meet with these moral monsters now and then – it is difficult to conceive how they came to exist here, or what there is in them capable of existence hereafter. They seem to be on the outside of everything; and nothing wearies the soul more than an attempt to comprehend them within its grasp.'

ELSPETH DAVIE
On Christmas Afternoon

A young boy, in the midst of a great Christmas Day party, suddenly came bursting out of one of the upper rooms of the house and began to descend a long flight of stairs. The screams of the children, snapping off as the door shut behind him, seemed to propel him down the first few steps and almost sent him headlong down the rest, for his hands were pressed hard over his ears and his eyes were screwed tight shut. His panic had been sudden and overwhelming. For a moment the whole house, vibrating and jangling with light and noise, had become for him unstable, like a huge stone slipping out of place into some dangerous position. Now, in the comparative silence of the staircase he waited for it to right itself, steadying his hand on the banisters and looking out of the long hall window into the garden, where the trees stood absolutely still and black against the green afternoon sky. All the intense silence and coldness into which, in imagination, he could escape, lay beyond that window, and at the sight of that static world, breathing deeply its freezing air, he gradually grew calmer again. Cautiously now he began to make his way down towards the room below, treading softly and glancing round to see that his flight from one world into another had not been noticed. But there was no one about, no movement except the lamps swaying a little as the thumping of feet began again from overhead.

Three parties were going on in that house. In the top room the children's party was in full swing; below that on the first floor the grown-ups had started to dance; and on the ground floor beside the dining-room elderly people had gathered together for safety against the excitement of the rest of the house. But this boy had missed the labels and the introductions; he had come in at the end of supper and afterwards had found himself swept up with the children to the highest room. Very soon he discovered that this, after all, was not the place where he should be. Reddening with shame, he discovered the length of his arms and his legs compared with the others. He could reach up and bring down balloons which had lodged on the highest ledges, or pull out the streamers twisted about the centre light. The little grace which he had got made him conspicuous in the dancing games where the other children could only hop, and his own silence, amid bursts of screaming, frightened him and made his heart beat violently as though he had indeed jumped and screamed harder than all the rest. Now, standing in the middle of the staircase, he brushed off the silvery dust which had fallen on his shoulder and sleeve from frosted decorations, trying in that gesture to brush off every trace of childishness before entering the room below. But when he got to the door he leaned a long time against it with his head upon his folded arms, feeling the drum pounding through his temples, hearing the dancers passing close to him with a sound like a mysterious breeze blowing close to the ground. Even outside the door he felt the moving air on his legs, and when he opened it the hair was lifted from his scalp by a hot wind – a sensation like that which he had experienced only in moments of intense joy or fear.

Dozens of couples were sliding quickly past down the length of the room – a long, narrow room like a hall, not glinting and sparkling with tinsel and shining balls like the place he had just left, but glowing in red light, with deep avenues of shadow down both sides. Great lights swathed in red paper hung from the ceiling, swaying with the vibration of the room, and enormous red and green paper balls dangled against the heads of the tallest dancers, who knocked them sideways with their fists, shouting and laughing. The boy began to walk carefully along one side where chairs were lined up, half in shadow. Stiff girls sat waiting here, staring in front of them and fingering, as though they were charms, those brooches and bracelets which they had unwrapped that morning and put on for the first time that afternoon. Now and then some fierce movement from the centre knocked the boy sideways against their legs and he saw their eyes stare up at him, reproachful but indifferent, because he was not yet a man, and not yet to be reckoned with. He longed to sit there with them, because he knew that they were out of the dance for ever and therefore safe; but as though aware of this thought they became quickly hostile. Even their view of the dance was blocked now, as they leaned this way and that behind him, craning their necks and raising sharp elbows like a crowd of flurried birds. He went quickly on.

Right at the end of the room in the opposite corner there was another door leading down to the dining-room, and towards this he slowly made his way. Long green fronds of streamer caught his shoulder, the hems of swirling silk frocks brushed against his legs, and gusts of air, smelling of powder and dust and singeing crêpe paper, made his head swim as he wound in and out of light and shadow along the slippery floor. Sometimes he got caught within the circle of the dance and couples slid about him, laughing and pressing him off with their elbows; and once with a great effort he broke through and stumbled off as far into shadow as he could, right in behind the row of chairs under the pillars of the room. But even here there were people. Men and women sat in pairs together on the floor against the wall, their heads turned towards one another, their legs stretched limply out in front of them. Even before he could see them clearly he was stepping clumsily across these legs, while their heads turned and they waited silently for him to go. His clumsy recoil from this territory of love-making made them aware it was a child who had intruded, and an odd one at that – a child who plainly showed in his face a disbelief in the happiness either of their world or his own. For a moment all whispering and kissing stopped as he went by, and they drew in their legs to let him pass. But the boy had only one thought now, to reach the door opposite by plunging blindly through the midst of the dancers underneath the orchestra at the top of the room. Over his head the saxophone and the drum were working up to a frenzied crescendo; the noise for a moment was so great it seemed to shatter the whole room, and then suddenly it ceased and through the strong drift of dancers returning to their seats he moved on with his head down. Occasionally somebody would stand in his way to take a look at him, and catching a glimpse of his face a woman asked:

'Is anything wrong?'

'Can't you see? He's trying to get back for a second helping,' replied her partner. They made way for him now, laughing good-naturedly and pushing him on, and he was able to make a flying leap for the door through the clear space in front of him. As though from a long distance he heard their laughter as it closed behind him.

The room which he now entered was a place set apart from everything that was going on in the rest of the house, cosy and secluded as a plush-lined box. It seemed to the elderly people who sat there that he had not seen them at all, even though to get through the room he had to wind his way through their armchairs. He moved like somebody in a dream, bumping against them, shifting cushions from under their elbows and catching the ends of knitting needles with his awkward movements; even the gossip was disturbed by his distracted muttering as he passed by. They leaned forward curiously to look at him as he approached the mirror above the fireplace, chafing their hands and pulling their wraps closer for a few minutes as he stood blocking out the heat. He was beside himself now, looking at the boy in the glass as he would at a stranger, shocked by the whiteness of the face, the anxious lips and black stricken eyes peering close to him, the dark hair all on end. Vaguely he saw the heads behind him, leaning together, but he did not look round. On his left, above a short flight of steps, was the last door he would need to pass through in that house; he knew that from the room below, free for the first time that day, he could make his escape.

But the room was not empty as he had imagined. Mr Barns, who stood at the other end of the dining-room beside the fire, could not see the boy's face clearly, but he imagined from his appearance that he must have frightened him. They faced one another down the length of a huge table, a magnificent wreck of a table, strewn with tangled heaps of decoration paper, cracker wrappings and burst balloons; ragged chrysanthemums hung askew from their vases, and against the white tablecloth big red and yellow jellies which had not been touched shimmered in glass dishes, and mounds of pink blancmange toppled and slit apart with every thump of the drum from the room above. All down the table there was a faint rattling of glasses and spoons and Mr Barns did not attempt to make himself heard until the music stopped. He was wearing a large Father Christmas robe, dusty and badly ripped up one side; and with one foot on a chair, twisted uncomfortably round, he was attempting to sew up this tear. When he looked up again the boy had moved down the room, and as he came into the light Mr Barns was aware that approaching him now was a strange being, a haunted, unnatural child who should have been shouting with joy like the rest of them, but because of some earthquake in the centre of his private world had landed just on the outside of normal experience. He was a child who wished to be hidden at once, captured or embraced – whatever would take him out of sight quickly and put him into darkness. Mr Barns had never seen quite this expression on a face before, and it occurred to him now as he saw it that this, then, was the real meaning of a displaced person.

Mr Barns felt extraordinarily shy for the first time in his life. More than ever now he felt that it had been particularly foolish of his hostess to choose him to play the part of the children's saint. He knew that he was not specially good with children, he had none of his own, and moreover he had always hoped to keep out of the way of the so-called difficult ones who had to be handled in a special way, known only to psychologists. The boy was beside him now, staring so hard with his black eyes that Mr Barns felt that perhaps he must appear in some way a ludicrous figure, recognized even by the boy as being thoroughly unsuited to the part.

'At the very last minute I find this enormous tear,' he explained rather severely. 'No doubt the last Santa Claus was afraid to tell our hostess. Moreover, when I come to put on the mask I find that half the beard has been torn away, and that means half my afternoon is to be spent searching the whole house for glue and cotton wool as well as the needle and thread. Luckily the cotton wool was easy; there was too much snow on top of the Christmas tree and I soon removed that.' He sat down and began to stitch again. As he had suspected, the boy said nothing, but sat down on a chair beside him. Gradually Mr Barns decided that he would simply forget about the child, that he would not even try to understand him, but let him sit by his side, half covered by the red cloak, until he had come round again. They sat in silence, listening to the music stopping and starting again, and now and then hearing faint thumps and screams from the top of the house. Sometimes the man glanced down at the boy and they would exchange a smile which was a little ironic, because they were both out of it all, and both, for different reasons which neither of them could put into words, glad to be out of it.

'Now for the great moment,' said Mr Barns suddenly, getting up and consulting his watch. It seemed that this was a moment which the whole house had also anticipated. The music had stopped some time ago, and now there was a tremendous shuffling of feet from above and a grating of chairs pushed back. 'Now they are bringing in the tree,' said Mr Barns, nervously buttoning up his gown. 'In a minute the children will come down.' He was putting on the mask and hood now, exchanging the tired and anxious face of middle age for that of a rosy, benevolent old man. The child was standing up now, looking at him as though at one stroke he had lost everything in his world. It was a desperate look, out of all proportion to anything which had gone before, and having in it the very essence of every change and loss in love. It made his sharp, small face look suddenly old and rather ugly. Now from the top of the house they could hear the door opening and a great rush of feet down the stairs, then sudden shouts of triumph as the tree came in view.

'I'm going up now,' said Mr Barns, going over to the great sack in the corner, 'but I'll need some help handing these out, and besides there's all the stuff on the tree as well. You'd be a good hand at that, I think. Are you coming up?' His question was casual, but he had removed his mask to ask it, and now he waited for the reply as he might await some decision of tremendous moment. Many expressions which he could not understand passed across the boy's face, as though he looked back not only through the hours which had just been, but through years, further back than any normal child had a right to remember. But when he met Mr Barns' eyes again he had returned to that present moment and place.

'Yes,' he replied, keeping his eyes fixed on the other, 'I'm coming up with you.'

Everybody had come from all parts of the house now to the dancing-room above. The room where the old people had sat was quite empty, and as they went through it they could hear the tremendous hum of excitement beyond them through the closed door. Mr Barns now opened this door, quietly pushing himself through; but at once there was a roof-raising yell of triumph, a tremendous prolonged roar of welcome. Mr Barns retreated for a moment, peering back a little anxiously through his eye-slits at the boy behind.

'All this is coming to you one day when you're grown up,' he said. 'You'll get this sort of welcome somewhere, mark my words, and without dressing up for it either.' He told himself, for the sake of his conscience, that though this had never been true for him or for any other person in his experience, it might possibly be true for this boy, whose eyes, in spite of his fear, shone with such astounding and terrifying hope. Together they went into the cheering room.

CHARLES DICKENS
A Christmas Tree

I have been looking on, this evening, at a merry company of children assembled round that pretty German toy, a Christmas Tree. The tree was planted in the middle of a great round table, and towered high above their heads. It was brilliantly lighted by a multitude of little tapers; and everywhere sparkled and glittered with bright objects. There were rosy-cheeked dolls, hiding behind the green leaves; and there were real watches (with movable hands, at least, and an endless capacity of being wound up) dangling from innumerable twigs; there were French-polished tables, chairs, bedsteads, wardrobes, eight-day clocks, and various other articles of domestic furniture (wonderfully made, in tin, at Wolverhampton), perched among the boughs, as if in preparation for some fairy house-keeping; there were jolly, broad-faced little men, much more agreeable in appearance than many real men – and no wonder, for their heads took off, and showed them to be full of sugar-plums; there were fiddles and drums; there were tambourines, books, work-boxes, paint-boxes, sweetmeat-boxes, peep-show boxes, and all kinds of boxes; there were trinkets for the elder girls, far brighter than any grown-up gold and jewels; there were baskets and pincushions in all devices; there were guns, swords, and banners; there were witches standing in enchanted rings of pasteboard, to tell fortunes; there were tee-totums, humming-tops, needle-cases, pen-wipers, smelling-bottles, conversation-cards, bouquet-holders; real fruit, made artificially dazzling with gold leaf; imitation apples, pears, and walnuts, crammed with surprises; in short, as a pretty child, before me, delightedly whispered to another pretty child, her bosom friend, 'There was everything, and more.' This motley collection of odd objects, clustering on the tree like magic fruit, and flashing back the bright looks directed towards it from every side – some of the diamond-eyes admiring it were hardly on a level with the table, and a few were languishing in timid wonder on the bosoms of pretty mothers, aunts, and nurses – made a lively realization of the fancies of childhood; and set me thinking how all the trees that grow, and all the things that come into existence on the earth, have their wild adornments at that well-remembered time.

Being now at home again, and alone, the only person in the house awake, my thoughts are drawn back, by a fascination which I do not care to resist, to my own childhood. I begin to consider, what do we all remember best upon the branches of the Christmas Tree of our own young Christmas days, by which we climbed to real life.

Straight, in the middle of the room, cramped in the freedom of its growth by no encircling walls or soon-reached ceiling, a shadowy tree arises; and, looking up into the dreamy brightness of its top – for I observe in this tree the singular property that it appears to grow downward towards the earth – I look into my youngest Christmas recollections!

All toys at first, I find. Up yonder, among the green holly and red berries, is the Tumbler with his hands in his pockets, who wouldn't lie down, but whenever he was put upon the floor, persisted in rolling his fat body about, until he rolled himself still, and brought those lobster eyes of his to bear upon me – when I affected to laugh very much, but in my heart of hearts was extremely doubtful of him. Close beside him is that infernal snuff-box, out of which sprang a demoniacal Counsellor in a black gown, with an obnoxious head of hair, and a red cloth mouth, wide open, who was not to be endured on any terms, but could not be put away either; for he used suddenly, in a highly magnified state, to fly out of Mammoth Snuff-boxes in dreams; when least expected. Nor is the frog with cobbler's wax on his tail, far off; for there was no knowing where he wouldn't jump; and when he flew over the candle, and came upon one's hand with that spotted back – red on a green ground – he was horrible. The cardboard lady in a blue-silk skirt, who was stood up against the candlestick to dance, and whom I see on the same branch, was milder, and was beautiful; but I can't say as much for the larger cardboard man, who used to be hung against the wall and pulled by a string; there was a sinister expression in that nose of his; and when he got his legs round his neck (which he very often did), he was ghastly, and not a creature to be alone with.

When did that dreadful Mask first look at me? Who put it on, and why was I so frightened that the sight of it is an era in my life? It is not a hideous visage in itself; it is even meant to be droll; why then were its stolid features so intolerable? Surely not because it hid the wearer's face. An apron would have done as much; and though I should have preferred even the apron away, it would not have been absolutely insupportable, like the mask. Was it the immovability of the mask? The doll's face was immovable, but I was not afraid of *her*. Perhaps that fixed and set change coming over a real face infused into my quickened heart some remote suggestion and dread of the universal change that is to come on every face, and make it still? Nothing reconciled me to it. No drummers, from whom proceeded a melancholy chirping on the turning of a handle; no regiment of soldiers, with a mute band, taken out of a box, and fitted, one by one, upon a stiff and lazy little set of lazy-tongs; no old woman, made of wires and a brown-paper composition, cutting up a pie for two small children; could give me a permanent comfort, for a long time. Nor was it any satisfaction to be shown the Mask, and see that it was made of paper, or to have it locked up and be assured that no one wore it. The mere recollection of that fixed face, the mere knowledge of its existence anywhere, was sufficient to awake me in the night all perspiration and horror, with, 'O I know it's coming! O the mask!'

I never wondered what the dear old donkey with the panniers – there he is! – was made of, then! His hide was real to the touch, I recollect. And the great black horse with the round red spots all over him – the horse that I could even get upon – I never wondered what had brought him to that strange condition, or thought that such a horse was not commonly seen at Newmarket. The four horses of no colour, next to him, that went into the waggon of cheeses, and could be taken out and stabled under the piano, appear to have bits of fur-tippet for their tails, and other bits for their manes, and to stand on pegs instead of legs, but it was not so when they were brought home for a Christmas present. They were all right, then; neither was their harness unceremoniously nailed into their chests, as appears to be the case now. The tinkling works of the music-cart, I *did* find out, to be made of quill tooth-picks and wire; and I always thought that little tumbler in his shirt sleeves, perpetually swarming up one side of a wooden frame, and coming down, head foremost, on the other, rather a weak-minded person – though good-natured; but the Jacob's Ladder, next him, made of little squares of red wood, that went flapping and clattering over one another, each developing a different picture, and the whole enlivened by small bells, was a mighty marvel and a great delight.

Ah! The Doll's house! – of which I was not proprietor, but where I visited. I don't admire the Houses of Parliament half so much as that stone-fronted mansion with real glass windows, and door-steps, and a real balcony – greener than I ever see now, except at watering-places; and even they afford but a poor imitation. And though it *did* open all at once, the entire house-front (which was a blow, I admit, as cancelling the fiction of a staircase), it was but to shut it up again, and I could believe. Even open, there were three distinct rooms in it: a sitting-room and bedroom, elegantly furnished, and best of all, a kitchen, with uncommonly soft fire-irons, a plentiful assortment of diminutive utensils – oh, the warming-pan! – and a tin man-cook in profile, who was always going to fry two fish. What Barmecide justice have I done to the noble feasts wherein the set of wooden platters figured, each with its own peculiar delicacy, as a ham or turkey, glued tight on to it, and garnished with something green, which I recollect as moss! Could all the Temperance Societies of these later days, united, give me such a tea-drinking as I have had through the means of yonder little set of blue crockery, which really would hold liquid (it ran out of the small wooden cask, I recollect, and tasted of matches), and which made tea, nectar. And if the two legs of the ineffectual little sugar-tongs did tumble over one another, and want purpose, like Punch's hands, what does it matter? And if I did once shriek out, as a poisoned child, and strike the fashionable company with consternation, by reason of having drunk a little teaspoon, inadvertently dissolved in too hot tea, I was never the worse for it, except by a powder!

Upon the next branches of the tree, lower down, hard by the green roller and miniature gardening-tools, how thick the books begin to hang. Thin books, in themselves, at first, but many of them, and with deliciously smooth covers of bright red or green. What fat black letters to begin with! 'A was an archer, and shot at a frog.' Of course he was. He was an apple-pie also, and there he is! He was a good many things in his time, was A, and so were most of his friends, except X, who had so little versatility that I never knew him to get beyond Xerxes or Xantippe – like Y, who was always confined to a Yacht or a Yew Tree; and Z condemned for ever to be a Zebra or a Zany. But, now, the very tree itself changes, and becomes a bean-stalk – the marvellous bean-stalk up which Jack climbed to the Giant's house! And now, those dreadfully interesting, double-headed giants, with their clubs over their shoulders, begin to stride along the boughs in a perfect throng, dragging knights and ladies home for dinner by the hair of their heads. And Jack – how noble, with his sword of sharpness, and his shoes of swiftness! Again those old meditations come upon me as I gaze up at him; and I debate within myself whether there was more than one Jack (which I am loth to believe possible), or only one genuine original admirable Jack, who achieved all the recorded exploits.

Good for Christmas time is the ruddy colour of the cloak, in which – the tree making a forest of itself for her to trip through, with her basket – Little Red Riding-Hood comes to me one Christmas Eve to give me information of the cruelty and treachery of that dissembling Wolf who ate her grandmother, without making any impression on his appetite, and then ate her, after making that ferocious joke about his teeth. She was my first love. I felt that if I could have married Little Red Riding-Hood, I should have known perfect bliss. But, it was not to be; and there was nothing for it but to look out the Wolf in the Noah's Ark there, and put him late in the procession on the table, as a monster who was to be degraded. O the wonderful Noah's Ark! It was not found seaworthy when put in a washing-tub, and the animals were crammed in at the roof, and needed to have their legs well shaken down before they could be got in, even there – and then, ten to one but they began to tumble out at the door, which was but imperfectly fastened with a wire latch – but what was *that* against it! Consider the noble fly, a size or two smaller than the elephant: the lady-bird, the butterfly – all triumphs of art! Consider the goose, whose feet were so small, and whose balance was so indifferent, that he usually tumbled forward, and knocked down all the animal creation. Consider Noah and his family, like idiotic tobacco-stoppers; and how the leopard stuck to warm little fingers; and how the tails of the larger animals used gradually to resolve themselves into frayed bits of string!

Hush! Again a forest, and somebody up in a tree – not Robin Hood, not Valentine, not the Yellow

Dwarf (I have passed him and all Mother Bunch's wonders, without mention), but an Eastern King with a glittering scimitar and turban. By Allah! two Eastern Kings, for I see another, looking over his shoulder! Down upon the grass, at the tree's foot, lies the full length of a coal-black Giant, stretched asleep, with his head in a lady's lap; and near them is a glass box, fastened with four locks of shining steel, in which he keeps the lady prisoner when he is awake. I see the four keys at his girdle now. The lady makes signs to the two kings in the tree, who softly descend. It is the setting-in of the bright Arabian Nights.

Oh, now all common things become uncommon and enchanted to me. All lamps are wonderful; all rings are talismans. Common flower-pots are full of treasure, with a little earth scattered on the top; trees are for Ali Baba to hide in; beef-steaks are to throw down into the Valley of Diamonds, that the precious stones may stick to them, and be carried by the eagles to their nests, whence the traders, with loud cries, will scare them. Tarts are made, according to the recipe of the Vizier's son of Bussorah, who turned pastry-cook after he was set down in his drawers at the gate of Damascus; cobblers are all Mustaphas, and in the habit of sewing up people cut into four pieces, to whom they are taken blindfold.

Any iron ring let into stone is the entrance to a cave which only waits for the magician, and the little fire, and the necromancy, that will make the earth shake. All the dates imported come from the same tree as that unlucky date, with whose shell the merchant knocked out the eye of the genie's invisible son. All olives are of the stock of that fresh fruit, concerning which the Commander of the Faithful overheard the boy conduct the fictitious trial of the fraudulent olive merchant; all apples are akin to the apple purchased (with two others) from the Sultan's gardener for three sequins, and which the tall black slave stole from the child. All dogs are associated with the dog, really a transformed man, who jumped upon the baker's counter, and put his paw on the piece of bad money. All rice recalls the rice which the awful lady, who was a ghoul, could only peck by grains, because of her nightly feasts in the burial-place. My very rocking-horse – there he is, with his nostrils turned completely inside-out, indicative of Blood! – should have a peg in his neck, by virtue thereof to fly away with me, as the wooden horse did with the Prince of Persia, in the sight of all his father's Court.

Yes, on every object that I recognize among those upper branches of my Christmas Tree, I see this fairy light! When I wake in bed, at daybreak, on the cold dark winter mornings, the white snow dimly beheld, outside, through the frost on the window-pane, I hear Dinarzade. 'Sister, sister, if you are yet awake, I pray you finish the history of the Young King of the Black Islands.' Scheherazade replies, 'If my lord the Sultan will suffer me to live another day, sister, I will not only finish that, but tell you a more wonderful story yet.' Then, the gracious Sultan goes out, giving no orders for the execution, and we all three breathe again.

At this height of my tree I begin to see, cowering among the leaves – it may be born of turkey, or of pudding, or mince pie, or of these many fancies, jumbled with Robinson Crusoe on his desert island, Philip Quarll among the monkeys, Sandford and Merton with Mr Barlow, Mother Bunch, and the Mask – or it may be the result of indigestion, assisted by imagination and over-doctoring – a prodigious nightmare. It is so exceedingly indistinct, that I don't know why it's frightful – but I know it is. I can only make out that it is an immense array of shapeless things, which appear to be planted on a vast exaggeration of the lazy-tongs that used to bear the toy soldiers, and to be slowly coming close to my eyes, and receding to an immeasurable distance. When it comes closest, it is worst. In connection with it I descry remembrances of winter nights incredibly long; of being sent early to bed, as a punishment for some small offence, and waking in two hours, with a sensation of having been asleep two nights; of the laden hopelessness of morning ever dawning; and the oppression of a weight of remorse.

And now, I see a wonderful row of little lights rise smoothly out of the ground, before a vast green curtain. Now, a bell rings – a magic bell, which still sounds in my ears unlike all other bells – and music plays, amidst a buzz of voices, and a fragrant smell of orange-peel and oil. Anon, the magic bell commands the music to cease, and the great green curtain rolls itself up majestically, and The Play begins! The devoted dog of Montargis avenges the death of his master, foully murdered in the Forest of Bondy; and a humorous Peasant with a red nose and a very little hat, whom I take from this hour forth to my bosom as a friend (I think he was a Waiter or an Hostler at a village Inn, but many years have passed since he and I have met), remarks that the sassigassity of that dog is indeed surprising; and evermore this jocular conceit will live in my remembrance fresh and unfading, overtopping all possible jokes, unto the end of time. Or now, I learn with bitter tears how poor Jane Shore, dressed all in white, and with her brown hair hanging down, went starving through the streets; or how George Barnwell killed the worthiest uncle that ever man had, and was afterwards so sorry for it that he ought to have been let off. Comes swift to comfort me, the Pantomime – stupendous Phenomenon! – when clowns are shot from loaded mortars into the great chandelier, bright constellation that it is; when

Harlequins, covered all over with scales of pure gold, twist and sparkle, like amazing fish; when Pantaloon (whom I deem it no irreverence to compare in my own mind to my grandfather) puts red-hot pokers in his pocket, and cries 'Here's somebody coming!' or taxes the Clown with petty larceny, by saying, 'Now, I sawed you do it!' when Everything is capable, with the greatest ease, of being changed into Anything; and 'Nothing is, but thinking makes it so'. Now, too, I perceive my first experience of the dreary sensation – often to return in after-life – of being unable, next day, to get back to the dull, settled world; of wanting to live for ever in the bright atmosphere I have quitted; of doting on the little Fairy, with the wand like a celestial Barber's Pole, and pining for a Fairy immortality along with her. Ah, she comes back, in many shapes, as my eye wanders down the branches of my Christmas Tree, and goes as often, and has never yet stayed by me!

Out of this delight springs the toy-theatre – there it is, with its familiar proscenium, and ladies in feathers, in the boxes! – and all its attendant occupation with paste and glue, and gum, and water colours, in the getting-up of The Miller and his Men, and Elizabeth, or the Exile of Siberia. In spite of a few besetting accidents and failures (particularly an unreasonable disposition in the respectable Kelmar, and some others, to become faint in the legs, and double up, at exciting points of the drama), a teeming world of fancies so suggestive and all-embracing, that, far below it on my Christmas Tree, I see dark, dirty, real Theatres in the day-time, adorned with these associations as with the freshest garlands of the rarest flowers, and charming me yet.

But hark! The Waits are playing, and they break my childish sleep! What images do I associate with the Christmas music as I see them set forth on the Christmas Tree? Known before all the others, keeping far apart from all the others, they gather round my little bed. An angel, speaking to a group of shepherds in a field; some travellers, with eyes uplifted, following a star; a baby in a manger; a child in a spacious temple, talking with grave men; a solemn figure, with a mild and beautiful face, raising a dead girl by the hand; again, near a city gate, calling back the son of a widow, on his bier, to life; a crowd of people looking through the opened roof of a chamber where he sits, and letting down a sick person on a bed, with ropes; the same, in a tempest, walking on the water to a ship; again, on a sea-shore, teaching a great multitude; again, with a child upon his knee, and other children round; again, restoring sight to the blind, speech to the dumb, hearing to the deaf, health to the sick, strength to the lame, knowledge to the ignorant; again, dying upon a

Cross, watched by armed soldiers, a thick darkness coming on, the earth beginning to shake, and only one voice heard, 'Forgive them, for they know not what they do.'

Still, on the lower and maturer branches of the Tree, Christmas associations cluster thick. School-books shut up; Ovid and Virgil silenced; the Rule of Three, with its cool impertinent inquiries, long disposed of; Terence and Plautus acted no more, in an arena of huddled desks and forms, all chipped, and notched, and inked; cricket-bats, stumps, and balls, left higher up, with the smell of trodden grass and the softened noise of shouts in the evening air; the tree is still fresh, still gay. If I no more come home at Christmas time, there will be boys and girls (thank Heaven!) while the World lasts; and they do! Yonder they dance and play upon the branches of my Tree, God bless them, merrily, and my heart dances and plays too!

And I *do* come home at Christmas. We all do, or we all should. We all come home, or ought to come home, for a short holiday – the longer, the better – from the great boarding-school, where we are for ever working at our arithmetical slates, to take, and give a rest. As to going a-visiting, where can we not go, if we will; where have we not been, when we would; starting our fancy from our Christmas Tree!

Away into the winter prospect. There are many such upon the tree! On, by low-lying, misty grounds, through fens and fogs, up long hills, winding dark as caverns between thick plantations, almost shutting out the sparkling stars; so, out on broad heights, until we stop at last, with sudden silence, at an avenue. The gate-bell has a deep, half-awful sound in the frosty air; the gate swings open on its hinges; and, as we drive up to a great house, the glancing lights grow larger in the windows, and the opposing rows of trees seem to fall solemnly back on either side, to give us place. At intervals, all day, a frightened hare has shot across this whitened turf; or the distant clatter of a herd of deer trampling the hard frost, has, for the minute, crushed the silence too. Their watchful eyes beneath the fern may be shining now, if we could see them, like the icy dewdrops on the leaves; but they are still, and all is still. And so, the lights growing larger, and the trees falling back before us, and closing up again behind us, as if to forbid retreat, we come to the house.

There is probably a smell of roasted chestnuts and other good comfortable things all the time, for we are telling Winter Stories – Ghost Stories, or more shame for us – round the Christmas fire; and we have never stirred, except to draw a little nearer to it. But, no matter for that. We came to the house, and it is an old house, full of great chimneys where wood is burnt on ancient dogs upon the hearth, and grim portraits (some of them with grim legends, too) lower distrustfully from the oaken panels of the walls. We are a middle-aged nobleman, and we make a generous supper with our host and hostess and their guests – it being Christmas-time, and the old house full of company – and then we go to bed. Our room is a very old room. It is hung with tapestry. We don't like the portrait of a cavalier in green, over the fireplace. There are great black beams in the ceiling, and there is a great black bedstead, supported at the foot by two great black figures, who seem to have come off a couple of tombs in the old baronial church in the park, for our particular accommodation. But, we are not a superstitious nobleman, and we don't mind. Well! we dismiss our servant, lock the door, and sit before the fire in our dressing-gown, musing about a great many things. At length we go to bed. Well! we can't sleep. We toss and tumble, and can't sleep. The embers on the hearth burn fitfully and make the room look ghostly. We can't help peeping out over the counterpane, at the two black figures and the cavalier – that wicked-looking cavalier – in green. In the flickering light they seem to advance and retire: which, though we are not by any means a superstitious nobleman, is not agreeable. Well! we get nervous – more and more nervous. We say 'This is very foolish, but we can't stand this; we'll pretend to be ill, and knock up somebody.' Well! we are just going to do it, when the locked door opens, and there comes in a young woman, deadly pale, and with long fair hair, who glides to the fire, and sits down in the chair we have left there, wringing her hands. Then, we notice that her clothes are wet. Our tongue cleaves to the roof of our mouth, and we can't speak; but we observe her accurately. Her clothes are wet; her long hair is dabbled with moist mud; she is dressed in the fashion of two hundred years ago; and she has at her girdle a bunch of rusty keys. Well! there she sits, and we can't even faint we are in such a state about it. Presently she gets up, and tries all the locks in the room with the rusty keys, which won't fit one of them; then, she fixes her eyes on the portrait of the cavalier in green, and says, in a low, terrible voice, 'The stags know it!' After that, she wrings her hands again, passes the bedside, and goes out at the door. We hurry on our dressing-gown, seize our pistols (we always travel with pistols), and are following, when we find the door locked. We turn the key, look out into the dark gallery; no one there. We wander away, and try to find our servant. Can't be done. We pace the gallery till daybreak; then return to our deserted room, fall asleep, and are awakened by our servant (nothing ever haunts *him*) and the shining sun. Well! we make a wretched breakfast, and all the company say we look queer. After breakfast, we go over the house with our host, and then we take him to the portrait of the cavalier in green, and then it all comes out. He was false to a young housekeeper once attached to that family, and famous for her beauty, who drowned herself in a pond, and whose body was discovered, after a long time, because the stags refused to drink of the water. Since which, it has been whispered that she traverses the house at midnight (but goes especially to that room where the cavalier in green was wont to sleep) trying the old locks with the rusty keys. Well! we tell our host of what we have seen, and a shade comes over his features, and he begs it may be hushed up; and so it is. But, it's all true; and we said so, before we died (we are dead now), to many responsible people.

There is no end to the old houses, with resounding galleries, and dismal state-bedchambers, and haunted wings shut up for many years, through which we may ramble, with an agreeable creeping up our back, and encounter any number of ghosts, but (it is worthy of remark perhaps) reducible to a very few general types and classes; for ghosts have little originality, and 'walk' in a beaten track. Thus, it comes to pass, that a certain room in a certain old hall, where a certain bad lord, baronet, knight, or gentleman, shot himself, has certain planks in the floor from which the blood *will not* be taken out. You may scrape and scrape, as the present owner has done, or plane and plane, as his father did, or scrub and scrub, as his grandfather did, or burn and burn with strong acids, as his great-grandfather did, but there the blood will still be – no redder and no paler – no more and no less – always just the same. Thus, in such another house there is a haunted door, that never will keep open; or another door that never will keep shut; or a haunted sound of a spinning-wheel, or a hammer, or a footstep, or a cry, or a sigh, or a horse's tramp, or the rattling of a chain. Or else, there is a turret-clock, which, at the midnight hour, strikes thirteen when the head of the family is going to die; or a shadowy, immovable black carriage which at such a time is always seen by somebody, waiting near the great gates in the stable-yard. Or thus, it came to pass how Lady Mary went to pay a visit at a large wild house in the Scottish Highlands, and, being fatigued with her long journey, retired to bed early, and innocently said, next morning, at the breakfast-table, 'How odd, to have so late a party last night, in this remote place, and not to tell me of it, before I went to bed!' Then, everyone asked Lady Mary what she meant. Then, Lady Mary replied, 'Why, all night long, the carriages were driving round and round the terrace, underneath my window!' Then, the owner of the house turned pale, and so did his Lady, and Charles Macdoodle of Macdoodle signed to Lady Mary to say no more, and every one was silent. After breakfast, Charles Macdoodle told Lady Mary that it was a tradition in the family that those rumbling carriages on the terrace betokened death. And so it proved, for, two months afterwards, the Lady of the mansion died. And Lady Mary, who was a Maid of Honour at Court, often told this story to the old Queen Charlotte; by this token that the old King always said, 'Eh, eh? What, what? Ghosts, ghosts? No such thing, no such thing!' And never left off saying so, until he went to bed.

Or, a friend of somebody's whom most of us know, when he was a young man at college, had a particular friend, with whom he made the compact that, if it were possible for the Spirit to return to this earth after its separation from the body, he of the twin who first died should reappear to the other. In course of time, this compact was forgotten by our friend; the two young men having progressed in life, and taken diverging paths that were wide asunder. But, one night, many years afterwards, our friend being in the North of England, and staying for the night in an inn, on the Yorkshire Moors, happened to look out of bed; and there, in the moonlight, leaning on a bureau near the window, steadfastly regarding him, saw his old college friend! The appearance being solemnly addressed, replied, in a kind of whisper, but very audibly, 'Do not come near me. I am dead. I am here to redeem my promise. I come from another world, but may not disclose its secrets!' Then, the whole form becoming paler, melted, as it were, into the moonlight, and faded away.

Or, there was the daughter of the first occupier of the picturesque Elizabethan house, so famous in our neighbourhood. You have heard about her? No! Why, *She* went out one summer evening at twilight, when she was a beautiful girl, just seventeen years of age, to gather flowers in the garden; and presently came running, terrified, into the hall to her father, saying, 'Oh, dear father, I have met myself!' He took her in his arms, and told her it was fancy, but she said, 'Oh no! I met myself in the broad walk, and I was pale and gathering withered flowers, and I turned my head, and held them up!' And, that night, she died; and a picture of her story was begun, though never finished, and they say it is somewhere in the house to this day, with its face to the wall.

Or, the uncle of my brother's wife was riding home on horseback, one mellow evening at sunset, when, in a green lane close to his own house, he saw a man standing before him, in the very centre of the narrow way. 'Why does that man in the cloak stand there!' he thought. 'Does he want me to ride over him?' But the figure never moved. He felt a strange sensation at seeing it so still, but slackened his trot and rode forward. When he was so close to it as almost to touch it with his stirrup, his horse shied, and the figure glided up the bank, in a curious, unearthly manner – backward, and without seeming to use its feet – and was gone. The uncle of my brother's wife, exclaiming, 'Good Heaven! It's my cousin Harry, from Bombay!' put spurs to his horse, which was suddenly in a profuse sweat, and, wondering at such a strange behaviour, dashed round to the front of his house. There, he saw the same figure, just passing in at the long French window of the drawing-room, opening on the ground. He threw his bridle to a servant, and hastened in after it. His sister was sitting there, alone. 'Alice, where's my cousin Harry?' 'Your cousin Harry, John?' 'Yes. From Bombay. I met him in the lane just now, and saw him enter here, this instant.' Not a creature had been seen by anyone; and in that hour and minute, as it afterwards appeared, this cousin died in India.

Or, it was a certain sensible old maiden lady, who died at ninety-nine, and retained her faculties to the last, who really did see the Orphan Boy; a story which has often been incorrectly told, but, of which the real truth is this – because it is, in fact, a story belonging to our family – and she was a connection of our family. When she was about forty years of age, and still an uncommonly fine woman (her lover died young, which was the reason why she never married, though she had many offers), she went to stay at a place in Kent, which her brother, an Indian-Merchant, had newly bought. There was a story that this place had once been held in trust, by the guardian of a young boy; who was himself the next heir, and who killed the young boy by harsh and cruel treatment. She knew nothing of that. It has been said that there was a Cage in her bedroom in which the guardian used to put the boy. There was no such thing. There was only a closet. She went to bed, made no alarm whatever in the night, and in the morning said composedly to her maid when she came in, 'Who is the pretty forlorn-looking child who has been peeping out of that closet all night?' The maid replied by giving a loud scream, and instantly decamping. She was surprised; but she was a woman of remarkable strength of mind, and she dressed herself and went downstairs, and closeted herself with her brother. 'Now, Walter,' she said, 'I have been disturbed all night by a pretty, forlorn-looking boy, who has been constantly peeping out of that closet in my room, which I can't open. This is some trick.' 'I am afraid not, Charlotte,' said he, 'for it is the legend of the house. It is the Orphan Boy. What did he do?' 'He opened the door softly,' said she, 'and peeped out. Sometimes, he came a step or two into the room. Then, I called to him, to encourage him, and he shrunk, and shuddered, and crept in again, and shut the door.' 'The closet has no communication, Charlotte,' said her brother, 'with any other part of the house, and it's nailed up.' This was undeniably true, and it took two carpenters a whole forenoon to get it open, for examination. Then, she was satisfied that she had seen the Orphan Boy. But, the wild and terrible part of the story is that he was also seen by three of her brother's sons, in succession, who all died young. On the occasion of each child being taken ill, he came home in a heat, twelve hours before, and said, Oh, Mamma, he had been playing under a particular oak-tree, in a certain meadow, with a strange boy – a pretty, forlorn-looking boy, who was very timid, and made signs! From fatal experience, the parents came to know that this was the Orphan Boy, and that the course of that child whom he chose for his little playmate was surely run.

Legion is the name of the German castles, where we sit up alone to wait for the Spectre – where we are shown into a room, made comparatively cheerful for our reception – where we glance round at the shadows, thrown on the blank walls by the crackling fire – where we feel very lonely when the village innkeeper and his pretty daughter have retired, after laying down a fresh store of wood upon the hearth, and setting forth on the small table such supper-cheer as a cold roast capon, bread, grapes, and a flask of old Rhine wine – where the reverberating doors close on their retreat, one after another, like so many peals of sullen thunder – and where, about the small hours of the night, we come into the knowledge of divers supernatural mysteries. Legion is the name of the haunted German students, in whose society we draw yet nearer to the fire, while the schoolboy in the corner opens his eyes wide and round, and flies off the footstool he has chosen for his seat, when the door accidentally blows open. Vast is the crop of such fruit, shining on our Christmas Tree; in blossom, almost at the very top; ripening all down the boughs!

Among the later toys and fancies hanging there – as idle often and less pure – be the images once associated with the sweet old Waits, the softened music in the night, ever unalterable! Encircled by the social thoughts of Christmas time, still let the benignant figure of my childhood stand unchanged! In every cheerful image and suggestion that the season brings, may the bright star that rested above the poor roof be the star of all the Christian World! A moment's pause, O vanishing tree, of which the lower boughs are dark to me as yet, and let me look once more! I know there are blank spaces on thy branches, where eyes that I have loved have shone and smiled; from which they are departed. But, far above, I see the raiser of the dead girl, and the Widow's Son; and God is good! If Age be hiding for me in the unseen portion of thy downward growth, O may I, with a grey head, turn a child's heart to that figure yet, and a child's trustfulness and confidence!

Now, the tree is decorated with bright merriment, and song, and dance, and cheerfulness. And they are welcome. Innocent and welcome be they ever held, beneath the branches of the Christmas Tree, which cast no gloomy shadow! But, as it sinks into the ground, I hear a whisper going through the leaves. 'This, in commemoration of the law of love and kindness, mercy and compassion. This, in remembrance of Me!'

MORLEY CALLAGHAN
A Very Merry Christmas

After midnight on Christmas Eve hundreds of people prayed at the crib of the Infant Jesus which was to the right of the altar under the evergreen-tree branches in St Malachi's church. That night there had been a heavy fall of wet snow, and there was a muddy path up to the crib. Both Sylvanus O'Meara, the old caretaker who had helped to prepare the crib, and Father Gorman, the stout, red-faced, excitable parish priest, had agreed it was the most lifelike tableau of the Child Jesus in a corner of the stable at Bethlehem they had ever had in the church.

But early on Christmas morning Father Gorman came running to see O'Meara, the blood all drained out of his face and his hands pumping up and down at his sides, and he shouted, 'A terrible thing has happened. Where is the Infant Jesus? The crib's empty.'

O'Meara, who was a devout, innocent, wondering old man, who prayed a lot and always felt very close to God in the church, was bewildered and he whispered, 'Who could have taken it? Taken it where?'

'Take a look in the crib yourself, man, if you don't believe me,' the priest said, and he grabbed the caretaker by the arm, marched him into the church and over to the crib and showed him that the figure of the Infant Jesus was gone.

'Someone took it, of course. It didn't fly away. But who took it, that's the question,' the priest said. 'When was the last time you saw it?'

'I know it was here last night,' O'Meara said, 'because after the midnight mass when everybody else had gone home I saw Mrs Farrel and her little boy kneeling up here, and when they stood up I wished them a merry Christmas. You don't think she'd touch it, do you?'

'What nonsense, O'Meara. There's not a finer woman in the parish. I'm going over to her house for dinner tonight.'

'I noticed that she wanted to go home, but the little boy wanted to stay there and keep praying by the crib; but after they went home I said a few prayers myself and the Infant Jesus was still there.'

Grabbing O'Meara by the arm the priest whispered excitedly, 'It must be the work of communists or atheists.' There was a sudden rush of blood to his face. 'This isn't the first time they've struck at us,' he said.

'What would communists want with the figure of the Infant Jesus?' O'Meara asked innocently. 'They wouldn't want to have it to be reminded that God was with them. I didn't think they could bear to have Him with them.'

'They'd take it to mock us, of course, and to desecrate the church. O'Meara, you don't seem to know much about the times we live in. Why did they set fire to the church?'

O'Meara said nothing because he was very loyal and he didn't like to remind the priest that the little fire they had in the church a few months ago was caused by a cigarette butt the priest had left in his pocket when he was changing into his vestments, so he was puzzled and silent for a while and then whispered, 'Maybe someone really wanted to take God away, do you think so?'

'Take Him out of the church?'

'Yes. Take Him away.'

'How could you take God out of the church, man? Don't be stupid.'

'But maybe someone thought you could, don't you see?'

'O'Meara, you talk like an old idiot. Don't you realize you play right into the hands of the atheists, saying such things? Do we believe an image is God? Do we worship idols? We do not. No more of that, then. If communists and atheists tried to burn this church once, they'll not stop till they desecrate it. God help us, why is my church marked out for this?' He got terribly excited and rushed away shouting, 'I'm going to phone the police.'

It looked like the beginning of a terrible Christmas Day for the parish. The police came, and were puzzled, and talked to everybody. Newspapermen came. They took pictures of the church and of Father Gorman, who had just preached a sermon that startled the congregation because he grew very eloquent on the subject of vandal outrages to the house of God. Men and women stood outside the church in their best clothes and talked very gravely. Everybody wanted to know what the thief would do with the image of the Infant Jesus. They all were wounded, stirred and wondering. There certainly was going to be something worth talking about at a great many Christmas dinners in the neighbourhood.

But Sylvanus O'Meara went off by himself and was very sad. From time to time he went into the church and looked at the empty crib. He had all kinds of strange thoughts. He told himself that if someone really wanted to hurt God, then just wishing harm to Him really hurt Him, for what other way was there of hurting Him? Last night he had had the feeling that God was all around the crib, and now it felt as if God wasn't there at all. It wasn't just that the image of the Infant Jesus was gone, but someone had done violence to that spot and had driven God away from it. He told himself that things could be done that would make God want to leave a place. It was very hard to know where God was. Of course, He would always be in the church, but where had that part of Him that had seemed to be all around the crib gone?

It wasn't a question he could ask the little groups of astounded parishioners who stood on the sidewalk outside the church, because they felt like wagging their fingers and puffing their cheeks out and talking about what was happening to God in Mexico and Spain.

But when they had all gone home to eat their Christmas dinners, O'Meara, himself, began to feel a little hungry. He went out and stood in front of the church and was feeling thankful that there was so much snow for the children on Christmas Day when he saw that splendid and prominent woman, Mrs Farrel, coming along the street with her little boy. On Mrs Farrel's face there was a grim and desperate expression and she was taking such long fierce strides that the five-year-old boy, whose hand she held so tight, could hardly keep up with her and pull his big red sleigh. Sometimes the little boy tried to lean back and was a dead weight and then she pulled his feet off the ground while he whimpered, 'Oh, gee, oh, gee, let me go.' His red snowsuit was all covered with snow as if he had been rolling on the road.

'Merry Christmas, Mrs Farrel,' O'Meara said. And he called to the boy, 'Not happy on Christmas day? What's the matter, son?'

'Merry Christmas, indeed, Mr O'Meara,' the woman snapped to him. She was not accustomed to paying much attention to the caretaker, a curt nod was all she ever gave him, and now she was far too angry and mortified to bother with him. 'Where's Father Gorman?' she demanded.

'Still at the police station, I think.'

'At the police station! God help us, did you hear that, Jimmie?' she said, and she gave such a sharp tug at the boy's arm that she spun him around in the snow behind her skirts where he cowered, watching O'Meara with a curiously steady pair of fine blue eyes. He wiped away a mat of hair from his forehead as he watched and waited. 'Oh, Lord, this is terrible,' Mrs Farrel said. 'What will I do?'

'What's the matter, Mrs Farrel?'

'I didn't do anything,' the child said. 'I was coming back here. Honest I was, mister.'

'Mr O'Meara,' the woman began, as if coming down from a great height to the level of an unimportant and simple-minded old man, 'maybe you could do something for us. Look on the sleigh.'

O'Meara saw that an old coat was wrapped around something on the sleigh, and stooping to lift it, he saw the figure of the Infant Jesus there. He was so delighted he only looked up at Mrs Farrel and shook his head in wonder and said, 'It's back and nobody harmed it at all.'

'I'm ashamed, I'm terribly ashamed, Mr O'Meara. You don't know how mortified I am,' she said, 'but the child really didn't know what he was doing. It's a disgrace to us, I know. It's my fault that I haven't trained him better, though God knows I've tried to drum respect for the church into him.' She gave such a jerk at the child's hand he slid on his knee in the snow keeping his eyes on O'Meara.

Still unbelieving, O'Meara asked, 'You mean he really took it from the church?'

'He did, he really did.'

'Fancy that. Why, child, that was a terrible thing to do,' O'Meara said, 'Whatever got into you?' Completely mystified he turned to Mrs Farrel, but he was so relieved to have the figure of the Infant Jesus back without there having been any great scandal that he couldn't help putting his hand gently on the child's head.

'It's all right, and you don't need to say anything,' the child said, pulling away angrily from his mother, and yet he never took his eyes off O'Meara, as if he felt there was some bond between them. Then he looked down at his mitts, fumbled with them and looked up steadily and said, 'It's all right, isn't it, mister?'

'It was early this morning, right after he got up, almost the first thing he must have done on Christmas Day,' Mrs Farrel said. 'He must have walked right in and picked it up and taken it out to the street.'

'But what got into him?'

'He makes no sense about it. He says he had to do it.'

'And so I did, 'cause it was a promise,' the child said. 'I promised last night, I promised God that if He would make Mother bring me a big red sleigh for Christmas I would give Him the first ride on it.'

'Don't think I've taught the child foolish things,' Mrs Farrel said. 'I'm sure he meant no harm. He didn't understand at all what he was doing.'

'Yes, I did,' the child said stubbornly.

'Shut up, child,' she said, shaking him.

O'Meara knelt down till his eyes were on a level with the child's and they looked at each other till they felt close together and he said, 'But why did you want to do that for God?'

''Cause it's a swell sleigh, and I thought God would like it.'

Mrs Farrel, fussing and red-faced, said, 'Don't you worry. I'll see he's punished by having the sleigh taken away from him.'

But O'Meara, who had picked up the figure of the Infant Jesus, was staring down at the red sleigh;

and suddenly he had a feeling of great joy, of the illumination of strange good tidings, a feeling that this might be the most marvellous Christmas Day in the whole history of the city, for God must surely have been with the child, with him on a joyous, carefree holiday sleigh ride, as he ran along those streets and pulled the sleigh. And O'Meara turned to Mrs Farrel, his face bright with joy, and said, commandingly, with a look in his eyes that awed her, 'Don't you dare say a word to him, and don't you dare touch that sleigh, do you hear? I think God did like it.'

FYODOR DOSTOEVSKY
The Beggar Boy at Christ's Christmas Tree

I am a novelist, and I believe I have made up this story. While I say 'I believe', I am certain that I did make it up. But somehow I cannot help feeling that this really happened somewhere, and must have happened on a Christmas eve, in a large city, on a terribly frosty day.

I can see a boy, a little boy, some six years old, or less. This boy awoke that morning in a cold and clammy cellar. He wore some kind of a loose coat, and shivered with cold. His breath issued from his mouth like white steam, and, sitting on the edge of a box, he found it amusing to emit this steam and watch it disappear. But he was terribly hungry. Several times that morning he had gone up to the cot, where, on a mat not thicker than a pancake and with some kind of a bundle for a pillow, his sick mother was lying. How did she come here? She had possibly come with her boy from some provincial town and had suddenly fallen ill. The landlady, who let 'corners' to lodgers, had been taken to the police station two days before; the lodgers had gone about their business and the only one left had been lying dead drunk for the last twenty-four hours, having thus anticipated the holiday. In another corner, groaning with rheumatism, lay an old woman of eighty, who had at one time been a children's nurse, but was now left to die alone. She was scolding and grumbling at the boy, so that he became afraid of going near her corner. He had found water to drink outside in the hall, but could not find a crust anywhere; and he tried a number of times to wake his mother. He began at last to fear the darkness; twilight had long set in, but no one made a light. Feeling his mother's face, he wondered why she did not move at all and was as cold as the wall. It was very cold here, he thought. He stood awhile, forgetting to remove his hand from the dead woman's shoulder, then he breathed on his small fingers to warm them, and, fumbling for his shabby cap on the cot, he softly groped his way out of the cellar. He would have gone sooner, but was scared of the big dog which had been howling all day outside a neighbour's door at the head of the stairs. Now the dog had left, and he went into the street.

Mercy, what a city! Never before had he seen anything like it. The town he had come from, the nights were always so pitch dark: just one lamp for the whole street. The little low, wooden houses were closed with shutters; the streets were deserted after dusk. People shut themselves up in the houses, and only packs of dogs, hundreds and thousands of them, barked and howled all night long. But he had been warm and had been given enough to eat, while there. . . . Lord! if he only *had* something to eat! And what a noise and bustle! What dazzling light, what crowds of people! . . . horses, carriages. . . . And the cold, the bitter cold! Frozen steam rose in clouds from the horses, out of their warmly breathing mouths and nostrils; through the flaky snow is heard the clanking of their hoofs against the stones, and there is such a pushing, jostling. . . . And, oh, Lord! he does so crave a morsel to eat! . . . And his tiny fingers all at once begin to hurt him so. A policeman passed him, and turned away, to avoid seeing the boy.

And now another street. What a wide one! Here they will surely be run over! How these people run, and race and shout! And the light – so much light! And, oh! what is this? A huge window. And behind the glass – a tree, so tall – reaching up to the ceiling. It is a Christmas tree, and on it ever so many little lights, gilt paper and apples, and little dolls and horses; and about the room children – so clean and well dressed – running, playing, laughing, and eating and drinking things. Now one little girl begins to dance with a little boy – such a pretty little girl! And you can hear music through the glass. And as the little boy in the street looks on in wonder, he too laughs, though his toes are beginning to ache, and his fingers are so red and stiff with cold that he cannot bend them, and it hurts to move them. Suddenly he remembered how they hurt him, and he began to cry, and ran on. But there again is another window, and behind it in the room another tree; there are tables laden with cakes – all sorts of them – red, yellow, with almonds; and four richly dressed young ladies sit there and give the cakes away to all who come; and the door is opened incessantly and people enter from the street. The little boy stole up to the door, suddenly opened it and went in. Oh dear, how they shouted and waved him back with their hands! One lady went up to him hastily, slipped a copper into his hand, and herself opened the door for him. How frightened he was! He dropped the coin, which rolled, clinking, down the steps: he could not bend his rigid, red fingers to hold it. He ran away as fast as he could, with no idea of where he was running. He felt like crying, but he was too frightened, and could only run, and meantime breathe on his hands to warm them. He was miserable; he felt so strange, so alone and forlorn. Suddenly . . . oh Lord, what is this now? An admiring crowd stands before a window, and behind the pane are three dolls, dressed in red and green gowns, looking just as if they were alive! One is a little old man who sits there, playing on a very large fiddle, and the other two stand close by and play on small fiddles; they regard each other and nod their heads in time while their lips move; they are speaking but one cannot hear them through the glass. At first the boy thought they were really alive, and when he realized they were dolls, he laughed. Never had he seen such dolls and never thought there could be such! He wanted to cry, yet had to laugh – the dolls were so very, very amusing! At this moment he felt that someone took hold of him from behind: a wicked, big boy who stood beside him, suddenly struck him on the head, snatched away his cap and tripped him. The little fellow stumbled to the ground, and people began to shout; numb with fright, he somehow picked himself up and ran, ran madly on, till, half unconsciously, he slipped into a gateway and found himself in a courtyard, where he cowered down behind a stack of wood. He felt safe there; it was dark, and 'they' would not find him.

He sat huddled up and could not catch his breath from fright. Suddenly, quite suddenly, he felt comfortable; hands and feet ceased to ache, and grew as warm as if he were sitting on a stove. Then he shuddered and gave a start; why, he had almost fallen asleep! How nice it would be to sleep here. 'I will rest here awhile, and go to look at the dolls again,' thought the boy, smiling to himself, adding: 'Just as though they are alive!' . . . Then it seemed to him that he heard his mother singing. 'Mother, I am asleep; it is so nice to sleep here!'

'Come to my Christmas tree, little boy!' a gentle voice whispered near him.

At first he thought it was his mother; but it was not she. Who is it then that calls him? He cannot see; but someone is bending over him; embraces him in the dark. He puts forth his hands . . . and lo! what a flood of bright light! . . . And oh! what a tree! But no, it cannot be; he has never seen such trees. . . . *Where* is he, now? Shining radiance everywhere, and so many, many little dolls all around him. . . . But no! they are not dolls; these are all little boys and little girls, so pretty and bright, dancing, flying, and they crowd around him and kiss him, and, as he gazes, he sees his mother looking at him, laughing happily.

'Mamma, Mamma! Oh, how nice it is here!' he exclaims, and again kisses the children, and wants to tell them at once about the dolls behind the shop window. He asks them: 'Who are you, little boys? Who are you, little girls?' He laughs and loves them all.

'This is Christ's Christmas tree,' they answer. 'On this day Christ always has a tree for such little children as have no tree of their own. . . .'

And he discovered that these boys and girls were all children like himself: that some had frozen to death in the baskets in which they had been deposited on doorsteps; others had died in wretched hovels, whither they had been sent from the Foundlings' Hospital; others again had starved to death at their mothers' dried-up breasts; had been suffocated in the foul air of third-class railroad carriages. And now, here they were all angels, Christ's guests, and He Himself was in their midst, extending His hands to them, blessing them and their poor, sinful mothers. . . . And the mothers stand there, a little apart, weeping; each one knows her little boy or girl; and the children fly up to them, and kiss them, and wipe away their tears with their tiny hands, and beg them not to weep, for they, the children, are so happy. . . .

And down below, on that Christmas morning, the porter found the body of a little boy who had hidden behind a stack of wood, and there frozen to death. His mother was also found. . . . She had died before him. They had met before God in heaven. . . .

Why in the world have I made up such a story, in this matter of fact diary of mine, which should treat only of real events? . . . But then, you see, I cannot help fancying that all this may have really happened – I mean what took place in the basement and behind the woodstack. As to Christ's Christmas tree, I can't tell you whether or not it may have really happened. But it is novelist's business to invent.

DAPHNE DU MAURIER
Happy Christmas

The Lawrence family lived in a large house just outside town. Mr Lawrence was a big heavy man, with a round face and a smile. He motored into town every day to his office, where he had a roll-top desk and three secretaries. During the day he used the telephone, and had a business lunch, and then used the telephone again. He made a lot of money.

Mrs Lawrence had fair hair and china-blue eyes. Mr Lawrence called her Kitten, but she was not helpless. She had a lovely figure and long fingernails, and she played bridge most afternoons. Bob Lawrence was ten. He was like Mr Lawrence, only smaller. He was fond of electric trains, and his father had got some men to fix up a miniature railway in the garden. Marigold Lawrence was seven. She was like her mother, only rounder. She had fifteen dolls. She kept breaking them somehow.

If you met them anywhere you would not recognize the Lawrences as being different from any other family. Perhaps that was the trouble. They were just a bit too much like all the rest. Life was a comfortable and an easy thing, which was, of course, very pleasant.

On Christmas Eve the Lawrence family did much the same as every other family. Mr Lawrence came home early from town so that he could stand around and watch the household get ready for tomorrow. He smiled more than usual and put his hands in his pockets and shouted, 'Look out, you damn fool!' when he tripped over the dog who was hiding behind some evergreen. Mrs Lawrence had cut bridge for once and was threading lanterns across the drawing-room. Actually it was the garden boy who threaded the lanterns, but Mrs Lawrence stuck little frills of coloured paper round them and handed them to him, and as she was smoking all the time the smoke got in the garden boy's eyes, but he was too polite to brush it away. Bob Lawrence and Marigold Lawrence kept running round the drawing-room and jumping on to the sofas and chairs and calling out, 'What am I going to have tomorrow? Am I going to have a train? Am I going to have a doll?' until Mr Lawrence got fed up and said, 'If you don't stop that row you won't get anything,' but he said it in a way that did not mean much, and the children were not deceived.

It was just before the children's bedtime that Mrs Lawrence was called to the telephone. She said 'Damn!' and some more smoke got into the garden boy's eyes. Mr Lawrence picked up a piece of evergreen and stuck it behind a picture. He whistled cheerfully.

Mrs Lawrence was away five minutes, and when she came back her blue eyes were full of sparks and her hair was rumpled. She looked like a kitten. The kind you pick up and say 'Sweet Puss!' to and then quickly put down again.

'Oh, it's a bit thick, it really is,' she said, and for a moment the children thought she was going to cry.

'What the hell's the matter?' asked Mr Lawrence.

'It's that refugee officer for the district,' said Mrs Lawrence. 'You know – I told you the place was swarming with refugees. Well, like everybody else, I had to put our names down as receivers when the thing started, never thinking seriously that anything would happen. And now it has. We've got to take in a couple, here, tonight.'

Mr Lawrence stopped smiling. 'Look here,' he said, 'the refugee officer can't do that sort of thing to people without proper warning. Why didn't you tell him to go to blazes?'

'I did,' said Mrs Lawrence indignantly, 'and all he could say was that he was very sorry, but it was the same for everybody, and people in every house were having to do it, and he said something about a "compulsory measure" which I did not understand, but it sounded nasty.'

'They can't do it,' said Mr Lawrence, sticking out his jaw. 'I'll get on the phone to someone in authority, I'll see that officer is sacked, I'll go into town myself, I'll . . .'

'Oh, what's the use?' said Mrs Lawrence. 'Don't let's get ourselves all heated over it. You forget it's Christmas Eve and everyone's out of town by now. Anyway, the creatures are on their way, and we can't very well lock the door. I suppose I shall have to break it to the servants.'

'What will the refugees do?' clamoured the children excitedly. 'Will they want to take our things? Will they want our beds?'

'Of course not,' said Mrs Lawrence sharply. 'Don't be such little idiots!'

'Where are we going to put them?' asked Mr Lawrence. 'We shall have every room full as it is with the Dalys and the Collinses coming over tomorrow. You surely don't suggest we put them off now?'

'No fear,' said Mrs Lawrence, her blue eyes sparkling. 'That's one comfort, we can truthfully say the house *is* full. No, the refugees can have the room over the garage. It's been very dry up to now, so the damp won't have got through. There is a bed there that we turned out of the house two months ago – the springs had gone. But there's nothing wrong with it. And I think the servants have an oil stove they don't use.'

Mr Lawrence smiled. 'You've got it all taped, haven't you?' he said. 'No one can get the better of you, Kitten. Oh well, as long as it doesn't hurt us, I don't care.' He swooped down in sudden relief and picked up Marigold. 'Anyway, we won't let it spoil our Christmas, will we, honey?' he said. And he tossed Marigold in the air, and she shrieked with laughter.

'It's not fair,' said Bob Lawrence, his round face flushed. 'Marigold is younger than me and she wants to hang up the same size stocking. I'm eldest, I ought to have the biggest, oughtn't I?'

Mr Lawrence rumpled his son's hair. 'Be a man, Bob,' he said, 'and don't tease your sister. I've got something for you tomorrow better than any toy you'll find in your stocking.'

Bob stopped scowling. 'Is it something for my railway?' he asked eagerly.

Mr Lawrence winked and would not answer.

Bob began to jump up and down on his bed. 'My present's going to be bigger than Marigold's,' he shouted in triumph, 'much, much bigger.'

'It's not, it's not,' cried Marigold tearfully. 'Mine is just as nice, isn't it, Dad?'

Mr Lawrence called to the nurse, 'Come and quieten the kids, will you? I think they're getting too excited.' He laughed and went down the stairs.

Mrs Lawrence met him halfway. 'They've arrived,' she said. Her voice had a warning note.

'Well?' he asked.

She shrugged her shoulders and made a little face. 'Jews,' she said briefly – and went into the nursery.

Mr Lawrence said something, and then he straightened his tie and put on an expression that he considered right for refugees. It was a mixture of sternness and bravado. He went round the drive to the garage and climbed the rickety stairs.

'Ha, good evening!' he said in loud, jovial tones as he entered the room. 'Are you fixed up all right?'

The room was rather dim, for the one electric light bulb had not been dusted for many months and it hung in one corner, away from the bed and the table and the stove. The two refugees stared for a moment without speaking. The woman was sitting at the table, unpacking a basket, from which she brought a loaf of bread and two cups. The man was spreading a blanket over the bed, and when Mr Lawrence spoke he straightened his back and turned towards him.

'We are so grateful,' he said. 'so very grateful.'

Mr Lawrence coughed and half laughed. 'Oh, that's all right,' he said. 'No trouble at all.'

They were Jews and no mistake. The man's nose was enormous, and his skin that typical greasy yellow. The woman had large dark eyes, with shadows beneath them. She looked unhealthy.

'Er – anything else you want?' asked Mr Lawrence.

The woman answered this time. She shook her head. 'We want nothing,' she said. 'We are very tired.'

'Everywhere was full,' said the man. 'No one could take us in. It is most generous of you.'

'Not at all, not at all,' said Mr Lawrence, waving his hand. 'Good thing we had this room empty. You must have had a stiff time where you've been.'

They said nothing to this.

'Well,' said Mr Lawrence, 'if there's nothing more I can do, I'll say good night. Don't forget to turn the stove down if it smokes. And – er – if you should need more food or blankets or anything, just give a knock on the back door and ask the servants. Good night.'

'Good night,' they echoed, and then the woman added, 'A Happy Christmas to you.'

Mr Lawrence stared. 'Oh yes,' he said: 'Yes, of course. Thanks very much.'

He turned up the collar of his coat as he walked round to the front door. It was cold. There would be a sharp frost. The gong was just sounding for dinner as he went into the hall. The garden boy had finished stringing up the lanterns, and they fluttered from the ceiling with a jaunty air. Mrs Lawrence was mixing a drink at the table by the fire.

'Hurry up,' she called over her shoulder, 'dinner will be spoilt, and if there's anything I loathe it's lukewarm duck.'

'Kids asleep?' asked Mr Lawrence.

'I shouldn't think so,' said Mrs Lawrence. 'It's difficult to get them to settle on Christmas Eve. I gave them both some chocolate and told them to be quiet. Want a drink?'

Later, when they were undressing for the night, Mr Lawrence poked his head round from the dressing room, a toothbrush in his hand.

'Funny thing,' he said, 'that woman wished me a Happy Christmas. I never knew the Jews kept Christmas before.'

'I don't suppose she knows what it means,' said Mrs Lawrence, and she patted some skin food into her round smooth cheek.

One by one the lights in the house were extinguished. The Lawrence family slept. Outside the sky was bright with stars. And in the room over the garage there was one light burning.

★ ★ ★

'I say, gosh, just look at this, I've got an aeroplane as well as a new engine for my railway,' shouted Bob. 'Look, it works like a real one. Look at the propeller.'

'Have I got two things from Dad as well?' asked Marigold, fumbling feverishly amongst the litter of paper on her bed and she threw aside the large doll she had just unpacked. 'Nurse,' she shrieked, 'where's my other present from Dad?' Her cheeks were hot and flushed.

'Serves you right for being so greedy,' mocked Bob. 'Look what I've got.'

'I'll break your silly horrid plane,' said Marigold, and tears began to fall down her cheeks.

'You musn't quarrel on Christmas Day,' said Nurse, and she drew a small box triumphantly from the heap of waste paper. 'Look, Marigold, what's in here?'

Marigold tore aside the paper. Soon she held a glittering necklace in her hands. 'I'm a princess!' she shouted. 'I'm a princess!'

Bob threw her a glance of contempt. 'It's not very big,' he said.

Downstairs Mr and Mrs Lawrence were being served with their morning tea. The electric stove was lit, the curtains drawn, and the room was flooded with sunlight. The letters and the parcels remained unopened, though, for both Mr and Mrs Lawrence listened aghast to the tale that Anna, the servant, had to tell.

'I can't believe it, it's preposterous,' said Mr Lawrence.

'I can. It's just typical of the sort of thing these people do,' said Mrs Lawrence.

'Won't I give that refugee officer hell!' said Mr Lawrence.

'I don't suppose he knew,' said Mrs Lawrence. 'They took jolly good care not to let on that anything might happen. Well, we can't keep them here now, that's certain. There's no one here to look after the woman.'

'We must telephone for an ambulance and have them removed,' said Mr Lawrence. 'I thought the woman had a bad colour. She must be pretty tough to have stood it, all alone.'

'Oh, those sort of people have babies very easily,' said Mrs Lawrence. 'They scarcely feel it. Well, I'm very thankful they were in the garage room and not in the house. They can't have done much damage there.'

'And, Anna,' she called, as the maid was leaving the room, 'be sure and tell Nurse that the children are not to go near the garage until the ambulance has been.'

Then they settled down to the letters and parcels.

'We'll make everyone laugh at the story, anyway,' said Mr Lawrence. 'It will go down well with the turkey and the plum pudding.'

When they had breakfasted and had dressed, and the children had been in to tumble about on the beds and show their presents, Mr and Mrs Lawrence went round to the garage to see what could be done about the refugees. The children were sent up to the nursery to play with their new things, because, after all, what had happened was not very nice, as Nurse agreed with Mrs Lawrence. And besides, you never knew.

When they came to the garage they found a little crowd of servants in the yard talking. There were the cook, and the parlour man, and one of the housemaids, and the chauffeur, and even the garden boy.

'What's going on?' asked Mr Lawrence.

'They've cleared out,' said the chauffeur.

'How do you mean, cleared out?'

'The fellow went off while we were having breakfast and got hold of a taxi,' said the chauffeur. 'He must have gone to the stand at the end of the road. Never a word to any of us.'

'And we heard wheels by the back gate,' chimed in the cook, 'and he and the taxi driver were lifting the woman into the car.'

'The fellow asked for the name of a hospital, and we told him there was a Jewish hospital just before you get into town,' said the chauffeur. 'He said he was very sorry to have given us all this trouble. Cool sort of customer, hadn't turned a hair.'

'And the baby. We saw the baby,' giggled the housemaid, and then she blushed furiously for no reason.

'Yes,' said the cook, 'a proper little Jew, the image of his father.'

And then they all laughed and looked at one another rather foolishly.

'Well,' said Mr Lawrence, 'there's nothing more any of us can do, I suppose.'

The servants melted away. The excitement for the moment was over. There was the Christmas party to prepare for, and what with one thing and another they felt they had been run off their legs already, and it was only ten o'clock.

'We'd better have a look,' said Mr Lawrence jerking his head at the garage. Mrs Lawrence made a face and followed him.

They climbed the rickety stairs to the little dark room in the loft. There was no sign of disorder. The bed had been placed back against the wall, and the blanket was neatly folded at the foot. The chair and table were in the usual place. The window in the room had been opened to let in the fresh morning air. The stove had been turned out. Only one thing showed that the room had been used. On the floor, beside the bed, was a glass of cold water.

Mr Lawrence did not say anything. Mrs Lawrence did not say anything, either. They went back to the house and into the drawing-room. Mr Lawrence wandered to the window and looked out across the garden. He could see Bob's miniature railway at the far corner. Mrs Lawrence opened a parcel she had not seen at breakfast. Overhead, shouts and yells told that the children were either enjoying themselves or not.

'What about your golf? Weren't you meeting the others at eleven?' asked Mrs Lawrence.

Mr Lawrence sat down on the window seat. 'I don't feel very keen,' he said.

Mrs Lawrence put back the vanity case she had just drawn from sheet after sheet of tissue paper.

'Funny,' she said, 'I feel sort of flat too, not a bit Christmassy.'

Through the open door they could see the table in the dining room being prepared for lunch. The decorations looked fine, with the little bunches of flowers amidst the silver. Round the centre was a great heap of crackers.

'I really don't know what else we could have done,' said Mrs Lawrence suddenly.

Mr Lawrence did not answer. He arose and began walking up and down the room. Mrs Lawrence straightened the evergreen behind a picture.

'After all, they didn't ask for anything,' said Mrs Lawrence. 'The man would have said,' went on Mrs Lawrence, 'if the woman had been very ill, or the baby. I'm sure they were both all right. They are so tough, that race.'

Mr Lawrence took out a cigar from his waistcoat pocket and put it back again.

'They'll be much better off in the Jewish hospital than they would have been here,' said Mrs Lawrence, ' – proper nursing and everything. We couldn't possibly have coped with it. Besides, going off in a hurry like that, so independent, we did not have a chance to suggest a thing.'

Mr Lawrence picked up a book and then shut it. Mrs Lawrence kept twisting and untwisting the belt on her dress.

'Of course,' she said hurriedly, 'I shall go and enquire how they are and take fruit and things, and perhaps some warm woollies, and ask if there is anything else they want. I'd go this morning, only I have to take the children to church. . . .'

And then the door opened and the children came into the room.

'I've got my new necklace on,' said Marigold. 'Bob hasn't anything new to wear.' She pirouetted round on her toes. 'Hurry up, Mummy, we shall be late, and we shall miss seeing all the people come in.'

'I hope they sing "Hark the Herald Angels",' said Bob. 'We learnt the words in school and I shan't have to look at the book. Why was Jesus born in a stable, Dad?'

'There wasn't room for them at the inn,' said Mr Lawrence.

'Why, were they refugees?' said Marigold.

Nobody answered for a moment, and then Mrs Lawrence got up and tied her hair in front of the looking-glass.

'Don't ask such silly questions, darling,' she said.

Mr Lawrence threw open the window. Across the garden came the sound of the church bells. The sun shone on the clean white frost, turning it to silver. Mr Lawrence had a funny, puzzled look on his face.

'I wish . . . ' he began, 'I wish . . .' But he never finished what he was going to say, because the two cars carrying the Daly family and the Collins family drove in at the gate and up the drive, and the children with shouts of delight were running out on to the steps and calling, 'Happy Christmas, Happy Christmas!'

ANTON CHEKHOV
At Christmas

I

'Tell me what to write,' said Yegor as he dipped his pen in the ink.

Not for four years had Vasilisa seen her daughter. The daughter, Yefimya, had gone to St Petersburg with her husband after their wedding, and she had written home twice. But not a word had been heard of her after that, she might have vanished into thin air. Milking the cow at dawn, making up the stove, dreaming at night, the old woman had only one thing on her mind: how was Yefimya getting on, was she alive? Vasilisa ought to send a letter, but her old man couldn't write – and there was no one else to ask.

Well, when Christmas came round Vasilisa could bear it no longer, and went to see Yegor at the inn. This Yegor was the landlady's brother who had been hanging round that pub doing nothing ever since he had come home from the army. He was said to turn out a good letter if he was properly paid. Vasilisa first had a word with the pub cook, and then with the landlady, and finally with Yegor himself. A fifteen-copeck fee was agreed.

And now, in the pub kitchen on Boxing Day, Yegor sat at the table holding a pen. Vasilisa stood before him brooding. She had a careworn, grief-stricken air. Her old husband, Peter – very thin, tall, brown-pated – had come in with her and stood staring straight before him like a blind man. On the stove a pan of pork was frying. It hissed, it spurted, it even seemed to be saying 'flue', 'flu', 'flew' or some such word. The room was hot and stuffy.

'What shall I write?' Yegor repeated.

'None of that, now!' said Vasilisa with an angry and suspicious look. 'Don't you rush me. You ain't doing us no favour. You're being paid, ain't you? So you write "to our dear son-in-law Andrew and our only beloved daughter Yefimya our love, a low bow and our parental blessing which shall abide for ever and ever."'

'OK. Carry on shooting!'

'We also wish you a Happy Christmas. We are alive and well, and we wish the same to you from Our Lord, er, and Heavenly King.'

Vasilisa pondered, exchanged glances with the old man.

'We wish the same to you from Our Lord, er, and Heavenly King,' she repeated – and burst into tears.

That was all she could say. And yet, when she had lain awake at night thinking, a dozen letters hadn't seemed enough to say it all. Since the daughter and her husband had left, a great deal of water had flowed under the bridge, and the old people had lived a life of utter loneliness, sighing deeply of a night as if they had buried their daughter. So many things had happened in the village since then, what with all the weddings and funerals. How long the winters had seemed, how long the nights!

'It's hot in here,' said Yegor, unbuttoning his waistcoat. 'About seventy degrees, I reckon.

'All right, then – what else?' he asked.

The old people said nothing.

'What's your son-in-law's job?' asked Yegor.

'He was a soldier, sir, as you know,' answered the old man in a frail voice. 'He left the service same time as you. He was a soldier, but now he works in St Petersburg, like – in the hydropathetics. There's a doctor cures the sick with the waters, and he's a doorman at that doctor's institution.'

'It's all written here,' said the old woman, taking a letter out of her kerchief. 'This came from Yefimya, God knows when. Perhaps they ain't alive no more.'

Yegor reflected and wrote rapidly.

'At the present juncture,' he wrote, 'seeing as how destiny has been determined in the Soldiering Feild we advises you to look in the Regulations of Disciplinnary Penalties and the Criminal Law of the War Department and you will see in them said Laws the civilization of the Higher Ranks of the War Deppartment.'

After writing this, he read it out aloud while Vasilisa was thinking that he ought to write how miserable they had been last year, when their grain hadn't even lasted till Christmas and they'd had to sell the cow. She ought to ask for money, she ought to write that the old man was often poorly – and was bound, soon, to be called to his Maker.

But how could she put it in words? What did you say first and what next?

'Pay attention,' Yegor went on writing. 'In Volume Five of Milittary Regulations. Soldier is a general Term as is well known your most important Genneral and the least important Private is both called Soldiers.'

The old man moved his lips.

'It would be nice to see our grandchildren,' he said softly.

'What grandchildren?' the old woman asked, looking at him angrily. 'Perhaps there ain't none.'

'Ain't none? But perhaps there is. Who can tell?'

'By which you can judge,' Yegor hurried on, 'which enemy is Foreign and which Internnal the most important Internnal Enemy is Bacchus.'

The pen squeaked, making flourishes like fish-hooks on the paper. Yegor was in a hurry and read out each line several times. He sat on a stool, legs sprawling under the table: a smug, hulking, fat-faced, red-necked creature. He was the very soul of vulgarity – of vulgarity brash, overbearing, exultant, and proud of having been born and bred in a pub. That this indeed was vulgarity Vasilisa fully realized, though she could not put it into words, but only looked at Yegor angrily and suspiciously. His voice, his meaningless words, the heat, the stuffiness . . . they made her head ache and muddled her thoughts, so she said nothing, thought nothing, and only waited for that pen to stop squeaking. But the old man was looking at Yegor with absolute faith. He trusted them both: his old woman who had brought him here, and Yegor. And when he had mentioned the 'hydro-pathetics' institution just now, his faith – alike in that institution and in the curative power of 'the waters' – had been written all over his face.

Yegor finished, stood up and read out the whole letter from the beginning. Not understand-ing, the old man nodded trustingly.

'Pretty good, a smooth job,' said he. 'God bless you. Pretty good.'

They put three five-copeck pieces on the table and left the pub. The old man stared straight before him as if he was blind, absolute faith written on his face, but as they came out of the pub Vasilisa swung her fist at the dog.

'Ugly brute!' she said angrily.

The old woman got no sleep that night for worrying. At dawn she rose, said her prayers and set off for the station to post the letter – a distance of between eight and nine miles.

II

Dr B. O. Moselweiser's Hydro was open on New Year's Day, as on any ordinary day, the only difference being that Andrew the doorman wore a uniform with new galloons. His boots had an extra special shine and he wished everyone who came in a Happy New Year.

It was morning. Andrew stood by the door reading a newspaper. At exactly ten o'clock in came a general whom he knew – one of the regulars – followed by the postman.

'Happy New Year, sir,' said Andrew, helping the general off with his cloak.

'Thank you, my good fellow. Same to you.'

On his way upstairs the general nodded towards a door and asked a question which he asked every day, always forgetting the answer.

'What goes on in there?'

'Massage room, sir!'

When the general's steps had died away, Andrew examined the postal delivery and found one letter addressed to himself. He opened it, read several lines. Glancing at the newspaper, he sauntered to his room which was down here on the ground floor at the end of the passage. His wife Yefimya sat on the bed feeding a baby. Another child, the eldest, stood near her with his curly head on her lap while a third slept on the bed.

Entering his room, Andrew gave his wife the letter.

'This must be from the village.'

Then he went out, not taking his eyes off the newspaper, and paused in the corridor near his door. He could hear Yefimya read out the first lines in a quavering voice. After reading them she couldn't carry on – those few lines were quite enough for her, she was bathed in tears. Hugging and kissing her eldest child, she began to speak – crying or laughing, it was hard to say which.

'This is from Granny and Grandpa,' she said. 'From the village. May the Holy Mother and the Blessed Saints be with them. They have snow drifts right up to the roofs now, and the trees are white as white. The children are sliding on their tiny toboggans. And there's dear old bald Grandpa on the stove. And there's a little yellow dog. My lovely darlings.'

As he listened, Andrew remembered that his wife had given him letters three or four times, asking him to post them to the village, but some important business had always prevented him. He had not posted those letters, and they had been left lying around somewhere.

'There's little hares running about them fields,' Yefimya chanted, bathed in tears and kissing her boy. 'Grandpa is quiet and gentle, and Granny is also kind and loving. In the village they live a godly life and fear the Lord. There's a little church, with such nice peasants singing in the choir. Holy Mother, our protector, take us away from this place!'

Andrew came back to his room for a smoke before anyone else arrived, and Yefimya suddenly stopped talking, quietened down and wiped her eyes. Only her lips quivered. She was so afraid of him, oh dear she was! His footsteps, his glance . . . they made her tremble with fright. She dared not utter a word in his presence.

No sooner had Andrew lit a cigarette than there was a ring from upstairs. He put out his cigarette, adopted an expression of great solemnity, and ran to his front door.

The general was descending from aloft, pink and fresh from his bath.

'What goes on in there?' he asked, pointing at a door.

Andrew drew himself up to attention, and announced in a loud voice that it was the 'Charcot showers, sir!'

JOHN UPDIKE
The Carol Sing

Surely one of the natural wonders of Tarbox was Mr Burley at the Town Hall carol sing. How he would jubilate, how he would God-rest those merry gentlemen, how he would boom out when the male voices became Good King Wenceslas:

> Mark my footsteps, good my page;
> Tread thou in them boldly:
> Thou shalt find the winter's rage
> Freeze thy blood less co-*oh*-ldly.

When he hit a good 'oh', standing beside him was like being inside a great transparent Christmas ball. He had what you'd have to call a God-given bass. This year, we other male voices just peck at the tunes: Wendell Huddlestone, whose hardware store has become the pizza place where the dropouts collect after dark; Squire Wentworth, who is still getting up petitions to protect the marsh birds from the atomic power plant; Lionel Merson, lighter this year by about three pounds of gallstones; and that selectman whose freckled bald head looks like the belly of a trout; and that fireman whose face is bright brown all the year round from clamming; and the widow Covode's bearded son, who went into divinity school to avoid the draft; and the Bisbee boy, who no sooner was back from Vietnam than he grew a beard and painted his car every colour of the rainbow; and the husband of the new couple that moved this September into the Whitman place on the beach road. He wears thick glasses above a little mumble of a mouth tight as a keyhole, but his wife appears perky enough.

> The-ey lo-oked up and sa-haw a star,
> Shining in the east, beyond them far;
> And to the earth it ga-ave great light,
> And so it continued both da-hay and night.

She is wearing a flouncy little Christmassy number, red with white polka dots, one of those dresses so short that when she sits down on the old plush deacon's bench she has to help it with her hand to tuck under her bottom, otherwise it wouldn't. A lively bit of a girl with long thighs glossy as pond ice. She smiles nervously up over her cup of cinnamon-stick punch, wondering why she is here, in this dusty draughty public place. We must look monstrous to her, we Tarbox old-timers. And she has never heard Mr Burley sing, but she knows something is missing this year; there is something failed, something hollow. Hester Hartner sweeps wrong notes into every chord: arthritis – arthritis and indifference.

> The first good joy that Mary had,
>   It was the joy of one;
> To see the blessed Jesus Christ
>   When he was first her son.

The old upright, a Pickering, for most of the year has its keyboard turned to the wall, beneath the town zoning map, its top piled high with rolled-up plot plans filing for variances. The Town Hall was built, strange to say, as a Unitarian church, around 1830, but it didn't take around here, Unitarianism; the sea air killed it. You need big trees for a shady mystic mood, or at least a lake to see yourself in like they have over in Concord. So the town bought up the shell and ran a second floor through the air of the sanctuary, between the balconies: offices and the courtroom below, more offices and this hall above. You can still see the Doric pilasters along the walls, the top halves. They used to use it more; there were the Tarbox

Theatricals twice a year, and political rallies with placards and straw hats and tambourines, and get-togethers under this or that local auspice, and town meetings until we went representative. But now not even the holly the ladies of the Grange have hung around can cheer it up, can chase away the smell of dust and must, of cobwebs too high to reach and rats' nests in the hot-air ducts and, if you stand close to the piano, that faint sour tang of blueprints. And Hester lately has taken to chewing eucalyptus drops.

> And him to serve God give us grace,
> *O lux beata Trinitas.*

The little wife in polka dots is laughing now: maybe the punch is getting to her, maybe she's getting used to the look of us. Strange people look ugly only for a while, until you begin to fill in those tufty monkey features with a little history and stop seeing their faces and start seeing their lives. Regardless, it does us good, to see her here, to see young people at the carol sing. We need new blood.

> This time of the year is spent in good cheer,
> And neighbours together do meet,
> To sit by the fire, with friendly desire,
> Each other in love to greet.

Old grudges forgot are put in the pot,
All sorrows aside they lay;
The old and the young doth carol this song,
To drive the cold winter away.

At bottom it's a woman's affair, a chance in the darkest of months to iron some man-fetching clothes and get out of the house. Those old holidays weren't scattered around the calendar by chance. Harvest and seedtime, seedtime and harvest, the elbows of the year. The women do enjoy it; they enjoy jostle of almost any kind, in my limited experience. The widow Covode as full of rouge and purple as an old-time Scollay Square tart, when her best hope is burial on a sunny day, with no frost in the ground. Mrs Hortense broad as a barn door, yet her hands putting on a duchess's airs. Mamie Nevins sporting a sprig of mistletoe in her neck brace. They miss Mr Burley. He never married and was everybody's gallant for this occasion. He was the one to spike the punch and this year they let young Covode do it, maybe that's why Little Polka Dots can't keep a straight face and giggles across the music like a pruning saw.

Adeste, fideles,
Laeti triumphantes;
Venite, venite
In Bethlehem.

Still that old tussle, 'v' versus 'wenite', the 'th' as hard or soft. Education is what divides us. People used to actually resent it, the way Burley, with his education, didn't go to some city, didn't get out. Exeter, Dartmouth, a year at the Sorbonne, then thirty years of Tarbox. By the time he hit fifty he was fat and fussy. Arrogant, too. Last sing, he two or three times told Hester to pick up her tempo. 'Presto, Hester, not andante!' Never married, and never really worked. Burley Hosiery, that his grandfather had founded, was shut down and the machines sold South before Burley got his manhood. He built himself a laboratory instead and was always about to come up with something perfect: the perfect synthetic substitute for leather, the harmless insecticide, the beer can that turned itself into mulch. Some said at the end he was looking for a way to turn lead into gold. That was just malice. Anything high attracts lightning, anybody with a name attracts malice. When it happened, the papers in Boston gave him six inches and a photograph ten years old. 'After a long illness.' It wasn't a long illness, it was cyanide, the Friday after Thanksgiving.

> The holly bears a prickle,
> As sharp as any thorn,
> And Mary bore sweet Jesus Christ
> On Christmas day in the morn.

They said the cyanide ate out his throat worse than a blow-torch. Such a detail is satisfying but doesn't clear up the mystery. Why? Health, money, hobbies, that voice. Not having that voice makes a big hole here. Without his lead, no man dares take the lower parts; we just wheeze away at the melody with the women. It's as if the floor they put in has been taken away and we're standing in air, halfway up the old sanctuary. We peek around guiltily, missing Burley's voice. The absent seem to outnumber the present. We feel insulted, slighted. The dead turn their backs. The older you get, the more of them snub you. He was rude enough last year, Burley, correcting Hester's tempo. At one point, he even reached over, his face black with impatience, and slapped her hands that were still trying to make sense of the keys.

> Rise, and bake your Christmas bread:
> Christians, rise! The world is bare,
> And blank, and dark with want and care,
> Yet Christmas comes in the morning.

Well, why anything? Why do *we*? Come every year sure as the solstice to carol these antiquities that if you listened to the words would break your heart. Silence, darkness, Jesus, angels. Better, I suppose, to sing than to listen.

DYLAN THOMAS
A Child's Christmas in Wales

One Christmas was so much like another,
in those years around the sea-town corner now
and out of all sound except the distant speaking
of the voices I sometimes hear a moment before
sleep,
that I can never remember whether it snowed
for six days and six nights when I was twelve
or whether it snowed for twelve days and
twelve nights when I was six.

All the Christmases roll down toward
the two-tongued sea, like a cold and headlong moon
bundling down the sky that was our street;
and they stop at the rim of the ice-edged,
fish-freezing waves, and I plunge my hands in the
snow and bring out whatever I can find. In goes
my hand into that wool-white bell-tongued ball of
holidays resting at the rim of the carol-singing
sea, and out come Mrs Prothero and the firemen.

It was on the afternoon of the day
of Christmas Eve, and I was in Mrs Prothero's
garden, waiting for cats, with her son Jim.
It was snowing. It was always snowing at Christmas.
December, in my memory, is white as Lapland,
though there were no reindeers.
But there were cats. Patient, cold and callous,
our hands wrapped in socks, we waited
to snowball the cats. Sleek and long as jaguars
and horrible-whiskered, spitting and snarling,
they would slink and sidle over the white
back-garden walls, and the lynx-eyed hunters,
Jim and I, fur-capped and moccasined trappers
from Hudson Bay, off Mumbles Road, would hurl
our deadly snowballs at the green of their eyes.

The wise cats never appeared. We were so still,
Eskimo-footed arctic marksmen in the muffling
silence of the eternal snows – eternal,
ever since Wednesday – that we never heard
Mrs Prothero's first cry from her igloo at the
bottom of the garden. Or, if we heard it at all,
it was, to us, like the far-off challenge of our enemy
and prey, the neighbour's polar cat. But soon the
voice grew louder. 'Fire!' cried Mrs Prothero,
and she beat the dinner-gong.

And we ran down the garden, with the snowballs
in our arms, toward the house; and smoke,
indeed, was pouring out of the dining-room,
and the gong was bombilating, and Mrs Prothero
was announcing ruin like a town crier in Pompeii.
This was better than all the cats in Wales
standing on the wall in a row. We bounded into
the house, laden with snowballs, and stopped at
the open door of the smoke-filled room.

Something was burning all right;
perhaps it was Mr Prothero, who always slept
there after midday dinner with a newspaper
over his face. But he was standing in the middle
of the room, saying, 'A fine Christmas!'
and smacking at the smoke with a slipper.
'Call the fire brigade,' cried Mrs Prothero
as she beat the gong.

'They won't be there,' said Mr Prothero,
'it's Christmas.'

There was no fire to be seen, only clouds of smoke
and Mr Prothero standing in the middle of them,
waving his slipper as though he were conducting.

'Do something,' he said.

And we threw all our snowballs into the smoke –
I think we missed Mr Prothero – and ran out
of the house to the telephone box.

'Let's call the police as well,' Jim said.

'And the ambulance.'

'And Ernie Jenkins, he likes fires.'

But we only called the fire brigade, and soon
the fire engine came and three tall men in helmets
brought a hose into the house and Mr Prothero
got out just in time before they turned it on.
Nobody could have had a noisier Christmas Eve.
And when the firemen turned off the hose and
were standing in the wet, smoky room, Jim's aunt,
Miss Prothero, came downstairs and peered in
at them. Jim and I waited, very quietly, to hear
what
she would say to them. She said the right thing,
always. She looked at the three tall firemen in their
shining helmets, standing among the smoke and
cinders and dissolving snowballs, and she said:
'Would you like anything to read?'

Years and years and years ago, when I was a boy,
when there were wolves in Wales, and birds
the colour of red-flannel petticoats whisked past

the harp-shaped hills, when we sang and wallowed
all night and day in caves that smelt like Sunday
afternoons in damp front farmhouse parlours,
and we chased, with the jawbones of deacons,
the English and the bears, before the motor-car,
before the wheel, before the duchess-faced horse,
when we rode the daft and happy hills bareback,
it snowed and it snowed. But here a small boy says:
'It snowed last year, too. I made a snowman and
my brother knocked it down and I knocked my
brother down and then we had tea.'

'But that was not the same snow,' I say.
'Our snow was not only shaken from whitewash
buckets down the sky, it came shawling out of the
ground
and swam and drifted out of the arms and hands
and
bodies of the trees; snow grew overnight on the
roofs of the houses like a pure and grandfather
moss, minutely white-ivied the walls and settled on
the postman, opening the gate, like a dumb, numb
thunderstorm of white, torn Christmas cards.'

'Were there postmen then, too?'
'With sprinkling eyes and wind-cherried noses,
on spread, frozen feet they crunched up to the
doors and mittened on them manfully. But all that
the children could hear was a ringing of bells.'

'You mean that the postman went rat-a-tat-tat and the doors rang?'

'I mean that the bells that the children could hear were inside them.'

'I only hear thunder sometimes, never bells.'

'There were church bells, too.'

'Inside them?'

'No, no, no, in the bat-black, snow-white belfries,
tugged by bishops and storks. And they rang their tidings over the bandaged town, over the frozen foam of the powder and ice-cream hills, over the crackling sea. It seemed that all the churches boomed for joy under my window; and the weathercocks crew for Christmas, on our fence.'

'Get back to the postmen.'

'They were just ordinary postmen, fond of walking
and dogs and Christmas and the snow.
They knocked on the doors with blue knuckles. . . .'

'Ours has got a black knocker. . . .'

'And then they stood on the white Welcome mat in
the little, drifted porches and huffed and puffed,
making ghosts with their breath, and jogged from
foot to foot like small boys wanting to go out.'

'And then the Presents?'

'And then the Presents, after the Christmas box.
And the cold postman, with a rose on his
button-nose, tingled down the tea-tray-slithered run
of the chilly glinting hill. He went in his ice-bound
boots like a man on fishmonger's slabs. He wagged his
bag like a frozen camel's hump, dizzily turned the corner
on one foot, and, by God, he was gone.'

'Get back to the Presents.'

'There were the Useful Presents: engulfing mufflers
of the old coach days, and mittens made for giant
sloths; zebra scarfs of a substance like silky gum
that could be tug-o'-warred down to the galoshes;
blinding tam-o'-shanters like patchwork tea cosies
and bunny-suited busbies and balaclavas for victims
of head-shrinking tribes; from aunts who always

wore wool next to the skin there were moustached and
rasping vests that made you wonder why the aunts
had any skin left at all; and once I had a little
crocheted nose bag from an aunt now, alas,
no longer whinnying with us. And pictureless books
in which small boys, though warned with quotations
not to, *would* skate on Farmer Giles' pond
and did and drowned; and books that told me
everything about the wasp, except why.'

'Go on to the Useless Presents.'

'Bags of moist and many-coloured jelly babies
and a folded flag and a false nose and a tram-
conductor's cap and a machine that punched tickets
and rang a bell; never a catapult; once, by mistake
that no one could explain, a little hatchet;
and a celluloid duck that made, when you pressed it,
a most unducklike sound, a mewing moo that an
ambitious cat might make who wished to be a cow;
and a painting book in which I could make the grass,
the trees, the sea and the animals any colour

I pleased, and still the dazzling sky-blue sheep
are grazing in the red field under the
rainbow-billed and pea-green birds.

Hardboileds, toffee, fudge and allsorts, crunches,
cracknels, humbugs, glaciers, marzipan, and
butterwelsh for the Welsh. And troops of
bright tin soldiers who, if they could not fight,
could always run. And Snakes-and-Families
and Happy Ladders. And Easy Hobbi-Games
for Little Engineers, complete with instructions.

Oh, easy for Leonardo! And a whistle to make
the dogs bark to wake up the old man next door
to make him beat on the wall with his stick
to shake our picture off the wall.
And a packet of cigarettes: you put one
in your mouth and you stood at the corner
of the street and you waited for hours, in vain,
for an old lady to scold you for smoking
a cigarette, and then with a smirk you ate it.
And then it was breakfast under the balloons.'

'Were there Uncles like in our house?'

'There are always Uncles at Christmas.
The same Uncles. And on Christmas mornings,
with dog-disturbing whistle and sugar fags,
I would scour the swatched town for the news of

the little world, and find always a dead bird
by the white Post Office or by the deserted swings;
perhaps a robin, all but one of his fires out.
Men and women wading or scooping back from
chapel,
with taproom noses and wind-bussed cheeks,
all albinos, huddled their stiff black jarring
feathers against the irreligious snow.

Mistletoe hung from the gas brackets in all
the front parlours; there was sherry and walnuts
and bottled beer and crackers by the dessert-
spoons;
and cats in their fur-abouts watched the fires;
and the high-heaped fire spat, all ready for
the chestnuts and the mulling pokers.

Some few large men sat in the front parlours,
without their collars, Uncles almost certainly,
trying their new cigars, holding them out
judiciously at arm's length, returning them
to their mouths, coughing, then holding them
out
again as though waiting for the explosion;
and some few small Aunts, not wanted in the
kitchen,
nor anywhere else for that matter, sat on the
very edges of their chairs, poised and brittle,
afraid to break, like faded cups and saucers.'

Not many those mornings trod the piling streets:
an old man always, fawn-bowlered, yellow-gloved
and, at this time of year, with spats of snow,
would take his constitutional to the white bowling
green and back, as he would take it wet or fine
on Christmas Day or Doomsday; sometimes two
hale
young men, with big pipes blazing, no overcoats
and wild-blown scarfs, would trudge, unspeaking,
down to the forlorn sea, to work up an appetite,
to blow away the fumes, who knows, to walk
into the waves until nothing of them was left
but the two curling smoke clouds of their
inextinguishable briars. Then I would be
slap-dashing home, the gravy smell of the dinners
of others, the bird smell, the brandy, the
pudding and mince, coiling up to my nostrils,
when
out of a snow-clogged side lane would come a boy
the spit of myself, with a pink-tipped cigarette
and the violet past of a black eye, cocky
as a bullfinch, leering all to himself.

I hated him on sight and sound, and would be
about to put my dog whistle to my lips
and blow him off the face of Christmas when
suddenly he, with a violet wink, put *his* whistle
to *his* lips and blew so stridently, so high,
so exquisitely loud, that gobbling faces,

their cheeks bulged with goose, would press
against their tinselled windows, the whole length
of the white echoing street. For dinner
we had turkey and blazing pudding, and after
dinner the Uncles sat in front of the fire,
loosened all buttons, put their large moist
hands over their watch chains, groaned a little
and slept. Mothers, aunts and sisters scuttled
to and fro, bearing tureens. Auntie Bessie, who
had already been frightened, twice, by a
clock-work mouse, whimpered at the sideboard
and had some elderberry wine. The dog was sick.
Auntie Dosie had to have three aspirins,
but Auntie Hannah, who liked port, stood in
the middle of the snowbound back yard, singing
like a big-bosomed thrush. I would blow up
balloons to see how big they would blow up to;
and, when they burst, which they all did,
the Uncles jumped and rumbled. In the rich
and heavy afternoon, the Uncles breathing
like dolphins and the snow descending,
I would sit among festoons and Chinese lanterns
and nibble dates and try to make a model man-o'-war,
following the Instructions for Little Engineers,
and produce what might be mistaken for
a sea-going tramcar.

Or I would go out, my bright new boots
squeaking, into the white world, on to the

seaward hill, to call on Jim and Dan and Jack
and to pad through the still streets, leaving
huge deep footprints on the hidden pavements.

'I bet people will think there's been hippos.'

'What would you do if you saw a hippo
coming down our street?'

'I'd go like this, bang! I'd throw him over
the railings and roll him down the hill and then
I'd tickle him under the ear and he'd wag his tail.'

'What would you do if you saw *two* hippos?'

Iron-flanked and bellowing he-hippos clanked
and battered through the scudding snow toward us
as we passed Mr Daniel's house.

'Let's post Mr Daniel a snowball through
his letter-box.'

'Let's write things in the snow.'

'Let's write, "Mr Daniel looks like a spaniel"
all over his lawn.'

Or we walked on the white shore.
'Can the fishes see it's snowing?'

The silent one-clouded heavens drifted on to the
sea.
Now we were snow-blind travellers lost on the
north hills, and vast dewlapped dogs, with flasks
round their necks, ambled and shambled up to us,
baying 'Excelsior'. We returned home through
the
poor streets where only a few children fumbled
with bare red fingers in the wheel-rutted snow
and cat-called after us, their voices fading away,
as we trudged uphill, into the cries of the dock
birds and the hooting of ships out in the whirling
bay. And then, at tea the recovered Uncles would
be jolly; and the ice cake loomed in the centre of
the table like a marble grave. Auntie Hannah
laced
her tea with rum, because it was only once a year.

Bring out the tall tales now that we told
by the fire as the gaslight bubbled like a diver.
Ghosts whooed like owls in the long nights
when I dared not look over my shoulder; animals
lurked in the cubbyhole under the stairs where the
gas meter ticked. And I remember that we went
singing carols once, when there wasn't the shaving
of a moon to light the flying streets. At the end
of a long road was a drive that led to a large
house, and we stumbled up the darkness of the
drive

that night, each one of us afraid, each one holding
a stone in his hand in case, and all of us too brave
to say a word. The wind through the trees
made noises as of old and unpleasant and maybe
webfooted men wheezing in caves. We reached
the black bulk of the house.

'What shall we give them? Hark the Herald?'

'No,' Jack said, 'Good King Wenceslas.
I'll count three.'

One, two, three, and we began to sing,
our voices high and seemingly distant in the
snow-felted darkness round the house that
was occupied by nobody we knew. We stood
close together, near the dark door.

> *Good King Wenceslas looked out*
> *On the Feast of Stephen . . .*

And then a small, dry voice, like the voice
of someone who has not spoken for a long time,
joined our singing: a small, dry, eggshell voice
from the other side of the door: a small dry voice
through the keyhole. And when we stopped
running
we were outside *our* house; the front room was
lovely;

balloons floated under the hot-water-bottle-gulping gas;
everything was good again and shone over the town.

'Perhaps it was a ghost,' Jim said.

'Perhaps it was trolls,' Dan said,
who was always reading.

'Let's go in and see if there's any jelly left,'
Jack said. And we did that.

Always on Christmas night there was music.
An uncle played the fiddle, a cousin sang
'Cherry Ripe', and another uncle sang 'Drake's Drum'.
It was very warm in the little house.
Auntie Hannah, who had got on to the parsnip
wine, sang a song about Bleeding Hearts and Death,
and then another in which she said her heart
was like a Bird's Nest; and then everybody
laughed again; and then I went to bed.
Looking through my bedroom window, out into
the moonlight and the unending smoke-coloured snow,
I could see the lights in the windows
of all the other houses on our hill and hear

the music rising from them up the long, steadily falling night. I turned the gas down, I got into bed. I said some words to the close and holy darkness, and then I slept.

STELLA GIBBONS
Christmas at Cold Comfort Farm

It was Christmas Eve. Dusk, a filthy mantle, lay over Sussex when the Reverend Silas Hearsay, Vicar of Howling, set out to pay his yearly visit to Cold Comfort Farm. Earlier in the afternoon he had feared he would not be Guided to go there, but then he had seen a crate of British Port-type wine go past the Vicarage on the grocer's boy's bicycle, and it could only be going, by that road, to the farmhouse. Shortly afterwards he was Guided to go, and set out upon his bicycle.

The Starkadders, of Cold Comfort Farm, had never got the hang of Christmas, somehow, and on Boxing Day there was always a run on the Howling Pharmacy for lint, bandages, and boracic powder. So the Vicar was going up there, as he did every year, to show them the ropes a bit. (It must be explained that these events took place some years before the civilizing hand of Flora Poste had softened and reformed the Farm and its rude inhabitants.)

After removing two large heaps of tussocks which blocked the lane leading to the Farm and thereby releasing a flood of muddy, icy water over his ankles, the Vicar wheeled his machine on towards the farmhouse, reflecting that those tussocks had never fallen there from the dung-cart of Nature. It was clear that someone did not want him to come to the place. He pushed his bicycle savagely up the hill, muttering.

The farmhouse was in silence and darkness. He pulled the ancient hell-bell (once used to warn excommunicated persons to stay away from Divine Service) hanging outside the front door, and waited.

For a goodish bit nothing happened. Suddenly a window far above his head was flung open and a voice wailed into the twilight –

'No! No! No!'

And the window slammed shut again.

'You're making a mistake, I'm sure,' shouted the Vicar, peering up into the webby thongs of the darkness. 'It's me. The Rev. Silas Hearsay.'

There was a pause. Then –

'Beant you postman?' asked the voice, rather embarrassed.

'No, no, of course not; come, come!' laughed the Vicar, grinding his teeth.

'I be comin',' retorted the voice. 'Thought it were postman after his Christmas Box.' The window slammed again. After a very long time indeed the door suddenly opened and there stood Adam Lambsbreath, oldest of the farm servants, peering up at the Reverend Hearsay by the light of a lonely rushdip (so called because you dipped it in grease and rushed to wherever you were going before it went out).

'Is anyone at home? May I enter?' enquired the Vicar, entering, and staring scornfully round the desolate kitchen, at the dead blue ashes in the grate, the thick dust on hanch and beam, the feathers blowing about like fun everywhere. Yet even here there were signs of Christmas, for a withered branch of holly stood in a shapeless vessel on the table. And Adam himself . . . there was something even more peculiar than usual about him.

'Are you ailing, man?' asked the Vicar irritably, kicking a chair out of the way and perching himself on the edge of the table.

'Nay, Rev., I be niver better,' piped the old man. '*The older the berry, The more it makes merry.*'

'Then why,' thundered the Vicar, sliding off the table and walking on tiptoe towards Adam with his arms held at full length above his head, 'are you wearing three of Mrs Starkadder's red shawls?'

Adam stood his ground.

'I mun have a red courtepy, master. Can't be Santa Claus wi'out a red courtepy,' he said. 'Iverybody knows that. Ay, the hand o' Fate lies heavy on us all, Christmas and all the year round alike, but I thought I'd bedight meself as Santa Claus, so I did, just to please me little Elfine. And this night at midnight I be goin' around fillin' the stockin's, if I'm spared.'

The Vicar laughed contemptuously.

'So that were why I took three o' Mrs Starkadder's red shawls,' concluded Adam.

'I suppose you have never thought of God in terms of Energy? No, it is too much to expect.' The Reverend Hearsay re-seated himself on the table and glanced at his watch. 'Where in Energy's name *is* everybody? I have to be at the Assembly Rooms to read a paper on *The Future of the Father Fixation* at eight, and I've got to feed first. If nobody's coming, I'd rather go.'

'Won't ee have a dram o' swede wine first?' a deep voice asked, and a tall woman stepped over the threshold, followed by a little girl of twelve or so with yellow hair and clear, beautiful features. Judith Starkadder dropped her hat on the floor and leant against the table, staring listlessly at the Vicar.

'No swede wine, I thank you,' snapped the Reverend Hearsay. He glanced keenly round the kitchen in search of the British Port-type, but there was no sign of it. 'I came up to discuss an article with you and yours. An article in *Home Anthropology*.'

''Twere good of ee, Reverend,' she said tiredly.

'It is called *Christmas: From Religious Festival to Shopping Orgy*. Puts the case for Peace and Good Will very sensibly. Both good for trade. What more can you want?'

'Nothing,' she said, leaning her head on her hand.

'But I see,' the Vicar went on furiously, in a low tone and glaring at Adam, 'that here, as everywhere else, the usual childish wish-fantasies are in possession. Stars, shepherds, mangers, stockings, fir-trees, puddings . . . Energy help you all! I wish you good night, and a prosperous Christmas.'

He stamped out of the kitchen, and slammed the door after him with such violence that he brought a slate down on his back tyre and cut it open, and he had to walk home, arriving there too late for supper before setting out for Godmere.

After he had gone, Judith stared into the fire without speaking, and Adam busied himself with scraping the mould from a jar of mincemeat and picking some things which had fallen into it out of a large crock of pudding which he had made yesterday.

Elfine, meanwhile, was slowly opening a small brown-paper parcel which she had been nursing, and at last revealed a small and mean-looking doll dressed in a sleazy silk dress and one undergarment that did not take off. This she gently nursed, talking to it in a low, sweet voice.

'Who gave you that, child?' asked her mother idly.

'I told you, mother. Uncle Micah and Aunt Rennett and Aunt Prue and Uncle Harkaway and Uncle Ezra.'

'Treasure it. You will not get many such.'

'I know, mother; I do. I love her very much, dear, dear Caroline,' and Elfine gently put a kiss on the doll's face.

'Now, missus, have ee got the Year's Luck? Can't make puddens wi'out the Year's Luck,' said Adam, shuffling forward.

'It's somewhere here. I forget –'

She turned her shabby handbag upside down, and there fell out on the table the following objects:

A small coffin-nail.

A menthol cone.

Three bad sixpences.

A doll's cracked looking-glass.

A small roll of sticking-plaster.

Adam collected these objects and ranged them by the pudding basin.

'Ay, them's all there,' he muttered. 'Him as gets the sticking-plaster'll break a limb; the menthol cone means as you'll be blind wi' headache, the bad coins means as you'll lose all yer money, and him as gets the coffin-nail will die afore the New Year. The mirror's seven years' bad luck for someone. Aie! In ye go, curse ye!' and he tossed the objects into the pudding, where they were not easily nor long distinguishable from the main mass.

'Want a stir, missus? Come, Elfine, my popelot, stir long, stir firm, your meat to earn,' and he handed her the butt of an old rifle, once used by Fig Starkadder in the Gordon Riots.

Judith turned from the pudding with what is commonly described as a gesture of loathing, but Elfine took the rifle butt and stirred the mixture once or twice.

'Ay, now tes all mixed,' said the old man, nodding with satisfaction. 'Tomorrer we'll boil un fer a good hour, and un'll be done.'

'Will an hour be enough?' said Elfine. 'Mrs Hawk-Monitor up at Hautcouture Hall boils hers for eight hours . . . and another four on Christmas Day.'

'How do ee know?' demanded Adam. 'Have ee been runnin' wi' that young goosepick Mus' Richard again?'

'You shut up. He's awfully decent.'

' 'Tisn't decent to run wi' a young popelot all over the downs in all weathers.'

'Well, it isn't any of your business, so shut up.'

After an offended pause, Adam said:

'Well, niver fret about puddens. None of 'em

here has iver tasted any puddens but mine, and they won't know no different.'

At midnight, when the farmhouse was in darkness save for the faint flame of a nightlight burning steadily beside the bed of Harkaway, who was afraid of bears, a dim shape might have been seen moving stealthily along the corridor from bedroom to bedroom. It wore three red shawls pinned over its torn nightshirt and carried over its shoulder a nosebag (the property of Viper the gelding), distended with parcels. It was Adam, bent on putting into the stockings of the Starkadders the presents which he had made or bought with his savings. The presents were chiefly swedes, beetroots, mangel-wurzels and turnips, decorated with coloured ribbons and strips of silver paper from tea packets.

'Ay,' muttered the old man, as he opened the door of the room where Meriam, the hired girl, was sleeping over the Christmas week. 'An apple for each will make 'em retch, a couple o' nuts will warm their wits.'

The next instant he stepped back in astonishment. There was a light in the room and there, sitting bolt upright in bed beside her slumbering daughter, was Mrs Beetle.

Mrs Beetle looked steadily at Adam, for a minute or two. Then she observed:

'Some 'opes.'

'Nay, niver say that, soul,' protested Adam, moving to the bedrail where hung a very fully fashioned salmon-pink silk stocking with ladders all down it. ''Tisn't so. Ee do know well that I looks on the maidy as me own child.'

Mrs Beetle gave a short laugh and adjusted a curler. 'You better not let Agony 'ear you, 'intin' I dunno wot,' said Mrs Beetle. ''Urry up and put yer rubbish in there, I want me sleep out; I got to be up at cock-wake ter-morrer.'

Adam put a swede, an apple and a small pot in the stocking and was tiptoeing away when Mrs Beetle, raising her head from the pillow, inquired:

'Wot's that you've give 'er?'

'Eye-shadow,' whispered Adam hoarsely, turning at the door.

'*Wot?*' hissed Mrs Beetle, inclining her head in an effort to hear. ''Ave you gorn crackers?'

'Eye-shadow. To put on the maidy's eyes. 'Twill give that touch o' glamour as be irresistible; it do say so on pot.'

'Get out of 'ere, you old trouble-maker! Don't she 'ave enough bother resistin' as it is, and then you go and give 'er . . . 'ere, wait till I –' and Mrs Beetle was looking around for something to throw as Adam hastily retreated.

'And I'll lay you ain't got no present fer me, ter make matters worse,' she called after him.

Silently he placed a bright new tin of beetle-killer on the washstand and shuffled away.

His experiences in the apartments of the other Starkadders were no more fortunate, for Seth was busy with a friend and was so furious at being interrupted that he threw his riding-boots at the old man, Luke and Mark had locked their door and could be heard inside roaring with laughter at Adam's discomfiture, and Amos was praying, and did not even get up off his knees or open his eyes as he discharged at Adam the goat-pistol which he kept ever by his bed. And everybody else had such enormous holes in their stockings that the small presents Adam put in them fell through on to the floor along with the big ones, and when the Starkadders got up in the morning and rushed round to the foot of the bed to see what Santa had brought, they stubbed their toes on the turnips and swedes and walked on the smaller presents and smashed them to smithereens.

So what with one thing and another everybody was in an even worse temper than usual when the family assembled round the long table in the kitchen for the Christmas dinner about half-past two the next afternoon. They would all have sooner been in some place else, but Mrs Ada Doom (Grandmother Doom, known as Grummer) insisted on them all being there, and as they did not want her to go mad and bring disgrace on the House of Starkadder, there they had to be.

One by one they came in, the men from the fields with soil on their boots, the women fresh from hennery and duck filch with eggs in their bosoms that they gave to Mrs Beetle who was just making the custard. Everybody had to work as usual on Christmas Day, and no one had troubled to put on anything handsomer than their usual workaday clouts stained with mud and plough-oil. Only Elfine wore a cherry-red jersey over her dark skirt and had pinned a spray of holly on herself. An aunt, a distant aunt named Mrs Poste, who lived in London, had unexpectedly sent her the pretty jersey. Prue and Letty had stuck sixpenny artificial posies in their hair, but they only looked wild and queer.

At last all were seated and waiting for Ada Doom.

'Come, come, mun we stick here like jennets i' the trave?' demanded Micah at last. 'Amos, Reuben, do ee carve the turkey. If so be as we wait much longer, 'twill be shent, and the sausages, too.'

Even as he spoke, heavy footsteps were heard approaching the head of the stairs, and everybody at once rose to their feet and looked towards the door.

The low-ceilinged room was already half in dusk, for it was a cold, still Christmas Day, without much light in the grey sky, and the only other illumination came from the dull fire, half-buried under a tass of damp kindling.

Adam gave a last touch to the pile of presents, wrapped in hay and tied with bast, which he had put round the foot of the withered thorn-branch that was the traditional Starkadder Christmas-tree, hastily rearranged one of the tufts of sheep's-wool that decorated its branches, straightened the raven's skeleton that adorned its highest branch in place of a fairy-doll or star, and shuffled into his place just as Mrs Doom reached the foot of the stairs, leaning on her daughter Judith's arm. Mrs Doom struck at him with her stick in passing as she went slowly to the head of the table.

'Well, well. What are we waiting for? Are you all mishooden?' she demanded impatiently as she seated herself. 'Are you all here? All? Answer me!' banging her stick.

'Ay, Grummer,' rose the low, dreary drone from all sides of the table. 'We be all here.'

'Where's Seth?' demanded the old woman, peering sharply on either side of the long row.

'Gone out,' said Harkaway briefly, shifting a straw in his mouth.

'What for?' demanded Mrs Doom.

There was an ominous silence.

'He said he was going to fetch something, Grandmother,' at last said Elfine.

'Ay. Well, well, no matter, so long as he comes soon. Amos, carve the bird. Ay, would it were a vulture, 'twere more fitting! Reuben, fling these dogs the fare my bounty provides. Sausages . . . pah! Mince-pies . . . what a black-bitter mockery it all is! Every almond, every raisin, is wrung from the dry, dying soil and paid for with sparse greasy notes grudged alike by bank and buyer. Come, Ezra, pass the ginger wine! Be gay, spawn! Laugh, stuff yourselves, gorge and forget, you rat-heaps! Rot you all!' and she fell back in her chair, gasping and keeping one eye on the British Port-type that was now coming up the table.

'Tes one of her bad days,' said Judith tonelessly. 'Amos, will you pull a cracker wi' me? We were lovers . . . once.'

'Hush, woman.' He shrank back from the proffered treat. 'Tempt me not wi' motters and paper caps. Hell is paved wi' such.' Judith smiled bitterly and fell silent.

Reuben, meanwhile, had seen to it that Elfine got the best bit off the turkey (which is not saying much) and had filled her glass with Port-type wine and well-water.

The turkey gave out before it got to Letty, Prue, Susan, Phoebe, Jane and Rennett, who were huddled together at the foot of the table, and they were making do with brussels-sprouts as hard as bullets drenched with weak gravy, and home-brewed braket. There was silence in the kitchen except for the sough of swallowing, the sudden suck of drinking.

'WHERE IS SETH?', suddenly screamed Mrs Doom, flinging down her turkey-leg and glaring round.

Silence fell; everyone moved uneasily, not daring to speak in case they provoked an outburst. But at that moment the cheerful, if unpleasant, noise of a motor-cycle was heard outside, and in another moment it stopped at the kitchen door. All eyes were turned in that direction, and in another moment in came Seth.

'Well, Grummer! Happen you thought I was lost!' he cried impudently, peeling off his boots and flinging them at Meriam, the hired girl, who cowered by the fire gnawing a sausage skin.

Mrs Doom silently pointed to his empty seat with the turkey-leg, and he sat down.

'She hev had an outhees. Ay, 'twas terrible,' reproved Judith in a low tone as Seth seated himself beside her.

'Niver mind, I ha' something here as will make her chirk like a mellet,' he retorted, and held up a large brown-paper parcel. 'I ha' been to the Post Office to get it.'

'Ah, gie it me! Aie, my lost pleasurings! Tes none I get, nowadays; gie it me now!' cried the old woman eagerly.

'Nay, Grummer. Ee must wait till pudden time,' and the young man fell on his turkey ravenously.

When everyone had finished, the women cleared away and poured the pudding into a large dusty dish, which they bore to the table and set before Judith.

'Amos? Pudding?' she asked listlessly. 'In a glass or on a plate?'

'On plate, on plate, woman,' he said feverishly, bending forward with a fierce glitter in his eyes. 'Tes easier to see the Year's Luck so.'

A stir of excitement now went through the company, for everybody looked forward to seeing everybody else drawing ill-luck from the symbols concealed in the pudding. A fierce, attentive silence fell. It was broken by a wail from Reuben –

'The coin – the coin! Wala wa!' and he broke into deep, heavy sobs. He was saving up to buy a tractor, and the coin meant, of course, that he would lose all his money during the year.

'Never mind, Reuben, dear,' whispered Elfine, slipping an arm round his neck. 'You can have the penny father gave me.'

Shrieks from Letty and Prue now announced that they had received the menthol cone and the sticking-plaster, and a low mutter of approval greeted the discovery by Amos of the broken mirror.

Now there was only the coffin-nail, and a ghoulish silence fell on everybody as they dripped pudding from their spoons in a feverish hunt for it; Ezra was running his through a tea-strainer.

But no one seemed to have got it.

'Who has the coffin-nail? Speak, you draf-saks!' at last demanded Mrs Doom.

'Not I.' 'Nay.' 'Niver sight nor snitch of it,' chorused everybody.

'Adam!' Mrs Doom turned to the old man. 'Did you put the coffin-nail into the pudding?'

'Ay, mistress, that I did – didn't I, Mis' Judith, didn't I, Elfine, my liddle lovesight?'

'He speaks truth for once, mother.'

'Yes, he did, Grandmother. I saw him.'

'*Then where is it?*' Mrs Doom's voice was low and terrible and her gaze moved slowly down the table, first on one side and then on the other, in search of signs of guilt, while everyone cowered over their plates.

Everyone, that is, except Mrs Beetle, who continued to eat a sandwich that she had taken out of a cellophane wrapper, with every appearance of enjoyment.

'Carrie Beetle!' shouted Mrs Doom.

'I'm 'ere,' said Mrs Beetle.

'Did you take the coffin-nail out of the pudding?'

'Yes, I did.' Mrs Beetle leisurely finished the last crumb of sandwich and wiped her mouth with a clean handkerchief. 'And will again, if I'm spared till next year.'

'You . . . you . . . you . . .' choked Mrs Doom, rising in her chair and beating the air with her clenched fists. 'For two hundred years . . . Starkadders . . . coffin-nails in puddings . . . and now . . . you . . . dare . . .'

'Well, I 'ad enough of it las' year,' retorted Mrs Beetle. 'That pore old soul Earnest Dolour got it, as well you may remember –'

'That's right. Cousin Earnest,' nodded Mark Dolour. 'Got a job workin' on the oil-field down Henfield way. Good money, too.'

'Thanks to me, if he 'as,' retorted Mrs Beetle. 'If I 'adn't put it up to you, Mark Dolour, you'd 'ave let 'im die. All of you was 'angin' over the pore old soul waitin' for 'im to 'and in 'is dinner pail, and Micah (wot's old enough to know better, 'eaven only knows) askin' 'im could 'e 'ave 'is wrist-watch if anything was to 'appen to 'im . . . it fair got me down. So I says to Mark, why don't yer go down and 'ave a word with Mr Earthdribble the undertaker in Howling and get 'im to tell Earnest it weren't a proper coffin-nail at all, it were a throw-out, so it didn't count. The bother we 'ad! Shall I ever fergit it! Never again, I says to meself. So this year there ain't no coffin-nail. I fished it out o' the pudden meself. Parss the water, please.'

'Where is it?' whispered Mrs Doom, terribly. 'Where is this year's nail, woman?'

'Down the –' Mrs Beetle checked herself, and coughed, 'down the well,' concluded Mrs Beetle firmly.

'Niver fret, Grummer, I'll get it up fer ee! Me and the water voles, we can dive far and deep!' and Urk rushed from the room laughing wildly.

'There ain't no need,' called Mrs Beetle after him. 'But anything to keep you an' yer rubbishy water voles out of mischief!' And Mrs Beetle went into a cackle of laughter, alternately slapping her knee and Caraway's arm, and muttering, 'Oh, cor, wait till I tell Agony! "Dive far and deep." Oh, cor!' After a minute's uneasy silence –

'Grummer.' Seth bent winningly towards the old woman, the large brown-paper parcel in his hand. 'Will you see your present now?'

'Aye, boy, aye. Let me see it. You're the only one that has thought of me, the only one.'

Seth was undoing the parcel, and now revealed a large book, handsomely bound in red leather with gilt lettering.

'There, Grummer. 'Tis the year's numbers o' *The Milk Producers' Weekly Bulletin and Cowkeepers' Guide*. I collected un for ee, and had un bound. Art pleased?'

'Ay. 'Tis handsome enough. A graceful thought,' muttered the old lady, turning the pages. Most of them were pretty battered, owing to her habit of rolling up the paper and hitting anyone with it who happened to be within reach. ''Tis better so. 'Tis heavier. Now I can *throw* it.'

The Starkadders so seldom saw a clean and handsome object at the farmhouse (for Seth was only handsome) that they now crept round, fascinated, to examine the book with murmurs of awe. Among them came Adam, but no sooner had he bent over the book than he recoiled from it with a piercing scream.

'Aie! . . . aie! aie!'

'What's the matter, dotard?' screamed Mrs Doom, jabbing at him with the volume. 'Speak, you kaynard!'

'Tes calf! Tes bound in calf! And tes our Pointless's calf, as she had last Lammastide, as was sold at Godmere to Farmer Lust!' cried Adam, falling to the floor. At the same instant, Luke hit Micah in the stomach, Harkaway pushed Ezra into the fire, Mrs Doom flung the bound volume of *The Milk Producers' Weekly Bulletin and Cowkeepers' Guide* at the struggling mass, and the Christmas dinner collapsed into indescribable confusion.

In the midst of the uproar, Elfine, who had climbed on to the table, glanced up at the window as though seeking help, and saw a laughing face looking at her, and a hand in a yellow string glove beckoning with a riding-crop. Swiftly she darted down from the table and across the room, and out through the half-open door, slamming it after her.

Dick Hawk-Monitor, a sturdy boy astride a handsome pony, was out in the yard.

'Hallo!' she gasped. 'Oh, Dick, I am glad to see you!'

'I thought you never would see me – what on earth's the matter in there?' he asked curiously.

'Oh, never mind them, they're always like that. Dick, do tell me, what presents did you have?'

'Oh, a rifle, and a new saddle, and a fiver – lots of things. Look here, Elfine, you mustn't mind, but I brought you –'

He bent over the pony's neck and held out a sandwich box, daintily filled with slices of turkey, a piece of pudding, a tiny mince-pie and a crystallized apricot.

'Thought your dinner mightn't be very –' he ended gruffly.

'Oh, Dick, it's lovely! Darling little . . . what is it?'

'Apricot. Crystallized fruit. Look here, let's go up to the usual place, shall we? – and I'll watch you eat it.'

'But you must have some, too.'

'Man! I'm stoked up to the brim now! But I dare say I could manage a bit more. Here, you catch hold of Rob Roy, and he'll help you up the hill.'

He touched the pony with his heels and it trotted on towards the snow-streaked Downs, Elfine's yellow hair flying out like a shower of primroses under the grey sky of winter.

O. HENRY
The Gift of the Magi

One dollar and eighty-seven cents. That was all. And sixty cents of it was in pennies. Pennies saved one and two at a time by bulldozing the grocer and the vegetable man and the butcher until one's cheek burned with the silent imputation of parsimony that such close dealing implied. Three times Della counted it. One dollar and eighty-seven cents. And the next day would be Christmas.

There was clearly nothing left to do but flop down on the shabby little couch and howl. So Della did it. Which instigates the moral reflection that life is made up of sobs, sniffles, and smiles, with sniffles predominating.

While the mistress of the home is gradually subsiding from the first stage to the second, take a look at the home. A furnished flat at $8 per week. It did not exactly beggar description, but it certainly had that word on the look-out for the mendicancy squad.

In the vestibule below was a letter-box into which no letter would go, and an electric button from which no mortal finger could coax a ring. Also appertaining thereunto was a card bearing the name 'Mr James Dillingham Young.'

The 'Dillingham' had been flung to the breeze during a former period of prosperity when its possessor was being paid $30 per week. Now, when the income was shrunk to $20, the letters of 'Dillingham' looked blurred, as though they were thinking seriously of contracting to a modest and unassuming D. But whenever Mr James Dillingham Young came home and reached his flat above he was called 'Jim' and greatly hugged by Mrs James Dillingham Young, already introduced to you as Della. Which is all very good.

Della finished her cry and attended to her cheeks with the powder rag. She stood by the window and looked out dully at a grey cat walking a grey fence in a grey backyard. Tomorrow would be Christmas Day, and she had only $1.87 with which to buy Jim a present. She had been saving every penny she could for months, with this result. Twenty dollars a week doesn't go far. Expenses had been greater than she had calculated. They always are. Only $1.87 to buy a present for Jim. Her Jim. Many a happy hour she had spent planning for something nice for him. Something fine and rare and sterling – something just a little bit near to being worthy of the honour of being owned by Jim.

There was a pier-glass between the windows of the room. Perhaps you have seen a pier-glass in an $8 flat. A very thin and very agile person may, by observing his reflection in a rapid sequence of longitudinal strips, obtain a fairly accurate conception of his looks. Della, being slender, had mastered the art.

Suddenly she whirled from the window and stood before the glass. Her eyes were shining brilliantly, but her face had lost its colour within twenty seconds. Rapidly she pulled down her hair and let it fall to its full length.

Now, there were two possessions of the James Dillingham Youngs in which they both took a mighty pride. One was Jim's gold watch that had been his father's and his grandfather's. The other was Della's hair. Had the Queen of Sheba lived in the flat across the airshaft, Della would have let her hair hang out the window some day to dry just to depreciate Her Majesty's jewels and gifts. Had King Solomon been the janitor, with all his treasures piled up in the basement, Jim would have pulled out his watch every time he passed, just to see him pluck at his beard from envy.

So now Della's beautiful hair fell about her, rippling and shining like a cascade of brown waters. It reached below her knee and made itself almost a garment for her. And then she did it up again nervously and quickly. Once she faltered for a minute and stood still while a tear or two splashed on the worn red carpet.

On went her old brown jacket; on went her old brown hat. With a whirl of skirts and with the brilliant sparkle still in her eyes, she fluttered out of the door and down the stairs to the street.

Where she stopped the sign read: 'Mme Sofronie. Hair Goods of All Kinds.' One flight up Della ran, and collected herself, panting. Madame, large, too white, chilly, hardly looked the 'Sofronie'.

'Will you buy my hair?' asked Della.

'I buy hair,' said Madame. 'Take yer hat off and let's have a sight at the looks of it.'

Down rippled the brown cascade.

'Twenty dollars,' said Madame, lifting the mass with a practised hand.

'Give it to me quick,' said Della.

Oh, and the next two hours tripped by on rosy wings. Forget the hashed metaphor. She was ransacking the stores for Jim's present.

She found it at last. It surely had been made for Jim and no one else. There was no other like it in any of the stores, and she had turned all of them inside out. It was a platinum fob chain simple and chaste in design, properly proclaiming its value by substance alone and not by meretricious ornamentation – as all good things should do. It was even worthy of The Watch. As soon as she saw it she knew that it must be Jim's. It was like him. Quietness and value – the description applied to both. Twenty-one dollars they took from her for it, and she hurried home with the 87 cents. With that chain on his watch Jim might be properly anxious about the time in any company. Grand as the watch was, he sometimes looked at it on the sly on account of the old leather strap that he used in place of a chain.

When Della reached home her intoxication gave way a little to prudence and reason. She got out her curling irons and lighted the gas and went to work repairing the ravages made by generosity added to love. Which is always a tremendous task, dear friends – a mammoth task.

Within forty minutes her head was covered with tiny, close-lying curls that made her look wonderfully like a truant schoolboy. She looked at her reflection in the mirror long, carefully, and critically.

'If Jim doesn't kill me,' she said to herself, 'before he takes a second look at me, he'll say I look like a Coney Island chorus girl. But what could I do – oh! what could I do with a dollar and eighty-seven cents?'

At seven o'clock the coffee was made and the frying-pan was on the back of the stove, hot and ready to cook the chops.

Jim was never late. Della doubled the fob chain in her hand and sat on the corner of the table near the door that he always entered. Then she heard his step on the stair away down on the first flight, and she turned white for just a moment. She had a habit of saying little silent prayers about the simplest everyday things, and now she whispered: 'Please God, make him think I am still pretty.'

The door opened and Jim stepped in and closed it. He looked thin and very serious. Poor fellow, he was only twenty-two – and to be burdened with a family! He needed a new overcoat and he was without gloves.

Jim stepped inside the door, as immovable as a setter at the scent of quail. His eyes were fixed upon Della, and there was an expression in them that she could not read, and it terrified her. It was not anger, nor surprise, nor disapproval, nor horror, nor any of the sentiments that she had been prepared for. He simply stared at her fixedly with that peculiar expression on his face.

Della wriggled off the table and went for him.

'Jim, darling,' she cried, 'don't look at me that way. I had my hair cut off and sold it because I couldn't have lived through Christmas without giving you a present. It'll grow out again – you won't mind, will you? I just had to do it. My hair grows awfully fast. Say "Merry Christmas!" Jim, and let's be happy. You don't know what a nice – what a beautiful, nice gift I've got for you.'

'You've cut off your hair?' asked Jim, laboriously, as if he had not arrived at that patent fact yet even after the hardest mental labour.

'Cut it off and sold it,' said Della. 'Don't you like me just as well, anyhow? I'm me without my hair, ain't I?'

Jim looked about the room curiously.

'You say your hair is gone?' he said with an air almost of idiocy.

'You needn't look for it,' said Della. 'It's sold, I tell you – sold and gone, too. It's Christmas Eve, boy. Be good to me, for it went for you. Maybe the hairs of my head were numbered,' she went on with a sudden serious sweetness, 'but nobody could ever count my love for you. Shall I put the chops on, Jim?'

Out of his trance Jim seemed quickly to wake. He enfolded his Della. For ten seconds let us regard with discreet scrutiny some inconsequential object in the other direction. Eight dollars a week or a million a year – what is the difference? A mathematician or a wit would give you the wrong answer. The magi brought valuable gifts, but that was not among them. This dark assertion will be illuminated later on.

Jim drew a package from his overcoat pocket and threw it upon the table.

'Don't make any mistake, Dell,' he said, 'about me. I don't think there's anything in the way of a haircut or a shave or a shampoo that could make me like my girl any less. But if you'll unwrap that package you may see why you had me going awhile at first.'

White fingers and nimble tore at the string and paper. And then an ecstatic scream of joy; and then, alas! a quick feminine change to hysterical tears and wails, necessitating the immediate employment of all the comforting powers of the lord of the flat.

For there lay The Combs – the set of combs, side and back, that Della had worshipped for long in a Broadway window. Beautiful combs, pure tortoiseshell, with jewelled rims – just the shade to wear in the beautiful vanished hair. They were expensive combs, she knew, and her heart had simply craved and yearned over them without the least hope of possession. And now they were hers, but the tresses that should have adorned the coveted adornments were gone.

But she hugged them to her bosom, and at length she was able to look up with dim eyes and a smile and say: 'My hair grows so fast, Jim!'

And then Della leaped up like a little singed cat and cried, 'Oh, oh!'

Jim had not yet seen his beautiful present. She held it out to him eagerly upon her open palm.

The dull precious metal seemed to flash with a reflection of her bright and ardent spirit.

'Isn't it a dandy, Jim? I hunted all over town to find it. You'll have to look at the time a hundred times a day now. Give me your watch. I want to see how it looks on it.'

Instead of obeying, Jim tumbled down on the couch and put his hands under the back of his head and smiled.

'Dell,' said he, 'let's put our Christmas presents away and keep 'em awhile. They're too nice to use just at present. I sold the watch to get the money to buy your combs. And now suppose you put the chops on.'

The magi, as you know, were wise men – wonderfully wise men – who brought gifts to the Babe in the manger. They invented the art of giving Christmas presents. Being wise, their gifts were no doubt wise ones, possibly bearing the privilege of exchange in case of duplication. And here I have lamely related to you the uneventful chronicle of two foolish children in a flat who most unwisely sacrificed for each other the greatest treasures of their house. But in a last word to the wise of these days, let it be said that of all who give gifts these two were the wisest. Of all who give and receive gifts, such as they are wisest. Everywhere they are wisest. They are the magi.

GEORGE MACKAY BROWN
The Lost Boy

There was one light in the village on Christmas Eve; it came from Jock Scabra's cottage, and he was the awkwardest old man that had ever lived in our village or in the island, or in the whole of Orkney.

I was feeling very wretched and very ill-natured myself that evening. My Aunty Belle had just been explaining to me after tea that Santa Claus, if he did exist, was a spirit that moved people's hearts to generosity and goodwill; no more or less.

Gone was my fat apple-cheeked red-coated friend of the past ten winters. Scattered were the reindeer, broken the sledge that had beaten such a marvellous path through the constellations and the Merry Dancers, while all the children of Orkney slept. Those merry perilous descents down the lum, Yule eve by Yule eve, with the sack of toys and books, games and chocolate boxes, had never really taken place at all. . . . I looked over towards our hearth, after my aunt had finished speaking: the magic had left it, it was only a place of peat flames and peat smoke.

I can't tell you how angry I was, the more I thought about it. How deceitful, how cruel, grown-ups were! They had exiled my dear old friend, Santa Claus, to eternal oblivion. The gifts I would find in my stocking next morning would have issued from Aunty Belle's 'spirit of generosity'. It was not the same thing at all. (Most of the year I saw little enough of that spirit of generosity – at Halloween, for example, she had boxed my ears till I saw stars that had never been in the sky, for stealing a few apples and nuts out of the cupboard, before 'dooking' time.)

If there was a more ill-tempered person than my Aunty Belle in the village, it was, as I said, old Jock Scabra, the fisherman with a silver ring in his ear and a fierce one-eyed tom cat.

His house, alone in the village, was lit that night. I saw it, from our front door, at eleven o'clock.

Aunty Belle's piece of common sense had so angered me, that I was in a state of rebellion and recklessness. No, I would *not* sleep. I would not even stay in a house from which Santa had been banished. I felt utterly betrayed and bereaved.

When, about half past ten, I heard rending snores coming from Aunty Belle's bedroom, I got out of bed stealthily and put my cold clothes on, and unlatched the front door and went outside. The whole house had betrayed me – well, I intended to be out of the treacherous house when the magic hour of midnight struck

The road through the village was deep in snow, dark except where under old Scabra's window the lamplight had stained it an orange colour. The snow shadows were blue under his walls. The stars were like sharp nails. Even though I had wrapped my scarf twice round my neck, I shivered in the bitter night.

Where could I go? The light in the old villain's window was entrancing – I fluttered towards it like a moth. How would such a sour old creature be celebrating Christmas Eve? Thinking black thoughts, beside his embers, stroking his wicked one-eyed cat.

The snow crashed like thin fragile glass under my feet.

I stood at last outside the fisherman's window. I looked in.

What I saw was astonishing beyond ghosts or trows.

There was no crotchety old man inside, no one-eyed cat, no ingrained filth and hung cobwebs. The paraffin lamp threw a circle of soft light, and all that was gathered inside that radiance was clean and pristine: the cups and plates on the dresser, the clock and ship-in-the-bottle and tea-caddies on the mantelpiece, the framed picture of Queen Victoria on the wall, the blue stones of the floor, the wood and straw of the fireside chair, the patchwork quilt on the bed.

A boy I had never seen before was sitting at the table. He might have been about my own age, and his head was a mass of bronze ringlets. On the table in front of him were an apple, an orange, a little sailing ship crudely cut from wood, with linen sails, probably cut from an old shirt. The boy – whoever he was – considered those objects with the utmost gravity. Once he put out his finger and touched the hull of the toy ship; as if it was so precious it had to be treated with special delicacy, lest it broke like a soap-bubble. I couldn't see the boy's face – only his bright hair, his lissom neck, and the gravity and joy that informed all his gestures. These were his meagre Christmas presents; silently he rejoiced in them.

Beyond the circle of lamp-light, were there other dwellers in the house? There may have been hidden breath in the darkened box bed in the corner.

I don't know how long I stood in the bitter night outside. My hands were trembling. I looked down at them – they were blue with cold.

Then suddenly, for a second, the boy inside the house turned his face to the window. Perhaps he had heard the tiny splinterings of snow under my boots, or my quickened heart-beats.

The face that looked at me was Jock Scabra's, but Jock Scabra's from far back at the pure source of his life, sixty winters ago, before the ring was in his ear and before bad temper and perversity had grained black lines and furrows into his face. It was as if a cloth had been taken to a tarnished web-clogged mirror.

The boy turned back, smiling, to his Christmas hoard.

I turned and went home. I lifted the latch quietly, not to awaken Aunty Belle – for, if she knew what I had been up to that midnight, there would have been little of her 'spirit of generosity' for me. I crept, trembling, into bed.

When I woke up on Christmas morning, the 'spirit of the season' had loaded my stocking and the chair beside the bed with boxes of sweets, a Guinness Book of Records, a digital watch, a game of space wars, a cowboy hat, and a 50 pence piece. Aunty Belle stood at my bedroom door, smiling. And, 'A merry Christmas,' she said.

Breakfast over, I couldn't wait to get back to the Scabra house. The village was taken over by children with apples, snowballs, laughter as bright as bells.

I peered in at the window. All was as it had been. The piratical old man sluiced the last of his breakfast tea down his throat from a cracked saucer. He fell to picking his black-and-yellow teeth with a kipper-bone. His house was like a midden.

The one-eyed cat yawned wickedly beside the new flames in the hearth.

ACKNOWLEDGEMENTS

ELIZABETH BOWEN: 'The Cheery Soul', reprinted from *The Demon Lover* (Jonathan Cape, 1945) © Elizabeth Bowen 1945, by permission of Jonathan Cape and the Estate of Elizabeth Bowen.

GEORGE MACKAY BROWN: 'The Lost Boy', reprinted from *Andrina* (Chatto & Windus/The Hogarth Press, 1983) © George Mackay Brown 1983, by permission of the author.

MORLEY CALLAGHAN: 'A Very Merry Christmas', reprinted from *The Short Stories of Morley Callaghan* (Macgibbon & Kee, 1963) © Morley Callaghan 1963, by permission of Curtis Brown.

ANTON CHEKHOV: 'At Christmas', reprinted from *The Steppe and Other Stories* by Anton Chekhov, translated and edited by Ronald Hingley (World's Classic, 1991; originally published in *The Oxford Chekhov*, vol.9, 1975) © Ronald Hingley 1975, by permission of Oxford University Press.

ELSPETH DAVIE: 'On Christmas Afternoon', reprinted from *The Traveller's Room* (Sinclair-Stevenson, 1992)